D0442392

the death of jayson porter

the death of jayson porter

by Jaime Adoff

JUMP AT THE SUN

HYPERION

New York

Copyright © 2008 by Jaime Adoff
All rights reserved. Published by Jump at the Sun/Hyperion Books for
Children, an imprint of Disney Book Group. No part of this book may be
reproduced or transmitted in any form or by any means, electronic or
mechanical, including photocopying, recording, or by any information
storage and retrieval system, without written permission from the publisher.
For information address Hyperion Books for Children, 114 Fifth Avenue,
New York, New York 10011-5690.
First Edition
1 3 5 7 9 10 8 6 4 2
Printed in the United States of America
Library of Congress Cataloging-in-Publication Data on file.
ISBN 978-1-4231-0691-3
Reinforced binding
Visit www.jumpatthesun.com

For Terri, my wife and best friend.
I'm so glad you decided to sit next to me
in 5th grade.

the death of jayson porter

after

I am a bullet
screaming to the ground.
The air rushing past me, so fast I can't breathe.
I am gasping.
The sound—like a 747 taking off in my eardrums.
Getting louder and louder.
The ground getting closer and closer.
This is supposed to get rid of my pain,
get rid of it forever.
This is my cure.
It
HURTS.
It wasn't supposed to hurt.
I was supposed to go unconscious.
I haven't passed out yet, and it hurts.
It hurts 'cause I can't breathe.
My chest collapsing against itself,

squeezing all my insides

OUT.

Squeezing *everything.*

The building an upside-down blur, balconies racing past
me.

Going even faster,

my eyes blasted open from the force of gravity.

I try to blink, but I can't.

My speed

much faster than I planned.

I flip over . . .

Feet first,

I start my reentry into the next life.

I really hope it's better than this one.

I see a woman pushing a stroller—

a man jogging—

people

living—

life.

before

CHAPTER ONE

What I do?
"OWWWW."

"You know what you did."

"OWWWW."

"Now clean it up. I want it all cleaned before I get home.
Understand? And if there is one spot left, there's going to
be hell to pay."

I flinch; expecting another. Recoiling from the attack.
Like a shotgun that's just been fired. Except I'm not the
gun. Mom is.

Mom. "Lizzie" to her drinking buddies.

All she knows is hittin'. My face gets red-hot. More embarrassed than pain. Makes me feel like a kid again.

Damn, I'm sixteen years old.

Mom keeps going. "Get rid of that smell, too. Put some of that Rug Fresh on it. I want it to smell as fresh as a baby's bottom. Do I make myself clear, Jayson? Do I?"

"Yes, ma'am," is all I can say. It's what I should say. It'll keep her calm knowin' that I'll mind her. Keep *her* calm; keep *me* safe.

"I'll be back late"

"Me and Layla are goin' to breakfast, then we're gonna run some errands and end up with a well-deserved girls' night out, so don't wait up."

I turn away from Mom's mouth. I try to be slick, but she catches me.

"Don't look at me like that. I *know* it's only eight thirty, but that's the difference between me and you—I'm an adult and you're a kid, so I can do what the hell I want. Now as for you, I don't want you up half the night. You don't sleep, you look terrible. I don't want my son looking like a zombie all the time. You're scaring off all my friends. People are startin' to talk. You know what Layla said the other day? She said the reason that Noreen don't come by anymore is because of you. *You*, Jayson. She called you *weird*. I won't have my friends calling my only son weird. Now go take a shower and get yourself together. You look like death warmed over. Lay'll be here any minute, and I don't want her seein' you lookin' like somethin' that just crawled out of a hole."

"Yes, ma'am."

Sunny Gardens

Layla—"Easy Lay" is what they call her. Sells herself on the weekends for extra cash. How else does Mom think she buys all those nice things? How does a cashier at SaveMart afford designer clothes and a Fiata XFX? She's got "sponsors."

That's what Trax says. Trax, my best friend. Both of us trapped in this hellhole. Twenty floors of delusions and despair.

Sunny Gardens. The last stop for single moms and their messed-up kids. The last stop before the streets. Sunny Gardens, where the elevators are always broke—but not as broke as the people livin' here. Where crack is bought and sold like they trade stocks on Wall Street. Shootin' with needles and guns while I'm tryin' to do my homework. Babies cryin' 'cause they hungry.

This is the *real* Third World.

Sunny Gardens, where there's always room for one more.

Come On Baby, Light My Fire
Speak of the devil.

"Hey, cutie, where you been hidin' yourself?" Layla comes
flyin' into the apartment like someone was chasin' her.
Almost trippin' over the stack of phone books by the
front door. I can smell the alcohol on her breath as soon
as she opens her mouth. She's wearin' a skimpy tank top
and too-short shorts, lookin' like an old-ass cheerleader
that lost her pom-poms.

"Hey, Lay, will you tell that boy to go clean himself up?
Maybe he'll listen to you, 'cause he sure as hell don't
listen to me." Mom is yelling from her bedroom, soundin'
like a scratchy old record, her voice skipping' on her
words.

Like I can't tell she's drinkin' back there. Mom and Layla
always like to get "tuned up" before they go out.

"You know it's only a matter of time before I get my
payday, just a matter of time." Layla starts talkin' to me,
completely ignoring what Mom said.

Layla Fay Morrison. One of Mom's *favorite* drinkin' buddies. Always talkin' so much trash. Thinkin' she's gonna get paid because, *according to Layla*, her mom was Jim Morrison's wife. Jim Morrison, from that psychedelic 1960s band The Doors.

Yeah, right. Everybody knows Layla changed her name to Morrison to try to get his money. Layla is sooo full of it. But Mom believes every word that crazy woman says.

Mom.

Her and Layla sure are a match.
For real.

I am lookin' *hard*

underneath the kitchen sink for stain remover. Can't ever find *anything* under this sink. Stuff is always all over the place in this apartment. Last night, Mom and that black dude were kickin' it. Dude spilled a whole plate of spaghetti on the carpet. Now Mom says I did it.

She was *so* wasted last night. So was that dude. Can't remember his name, bet Mom can't, either. Just some big brutha, with a shaved head. Mom loves the bruthas. And the bruthas *love* Mom. Who could resist a pretty blonde?

Dad couldn't. But all that's gone. . . .

Now it's just me and Mom. I know she doesn't want to be so mean to me, she just can't help it. Like she says, *"Sometimes I just have bad days."*

Bad days, gettin' more and more, but I know things will get better. I know Mom will get better. I know she loves me.

No matter what she says
or
how she hits
I know
she loves me.

Dad
Gerald David Porter.

I'm glad I look like him. I am smooth, honey-glazed face. Five foot ten, and I never have to shave. My hair is straighter than his, but I keep it cut short—close to my head. Both of us with chocolate freckle chips. Dad *used* to be a handsome dude. Kinda looked like a cross between that rapper MC Pretty and the boxer Darnell Fury.

Back in the day, Dad could fight. Said he was undefeated in the amateur ranks. Now he just hits the pipe. Hits it hard.

Problem is, that pipe hits back. Harder.

A-Bandoned, Florida

Nine a.m. Mom and Lay are tuned up and out the
door . . . Just another day in the hot hell of Bandon,
Florida. Me and Trax call it *A*-Bandoned. Wish a
hurricane would just wipe us off the map. No such luck.
We're too inland. Not close enough to the ocean.

My knees are getting rug burns from all this scrubbin',
and they're sweatin' too. *How do your knees sweat?*

I get up and go into the kitchen. *Dumb water always comes
out hot.* I grab some ice cubes out of
the freezer and walk over to the couch. This place is a
pigsty. Mom's got crap all over the place. It's not like
this apartment's that big to begin with. They call it a
two-bedroom, but it's really like a one-and-a-half. And
my room is the half.

You practically trip over the couch to get to the kitchen.
And two people can't even fit in the hallway going to the
bathroom. Always got leaks, and they never fix *anything*
around here. This place sucks—but it still ain't the worst
place in Bandon to live. They got some buildings in the
Heights that make the Gardens look like Trump Towers.
Now *that* is sad, for real.

I have to go in today

I jiggle the handle on the toilet to get it to flush and

practically get myself caught in my zipper. *Shit. Forgot I have to go in today.* Jigglin' the handle on the toilet reminds me of how I always have to jiggle the toilet handle at work. *Nothin' gets fixed at work, either.*

I race to the bedroom to throw on some clothes. I hate workin' Saturdays, especially in this heat. It's gonna be hot as hell in those RVs today.

Hot as *hell.*

Supposed to be there *right now.* I know Trax is already there, he's never late for work. I throw on some shorts and a semi-clean T-shirt, take an extra one for later.
Run into the kitchen,
grab
candy bar
fruit punch
backpack.

I'm gone.

CHAPTER TWO

No Wheels, No Girls

I take the only empty seat left. All the way in the back, on top of the engine. I should have waited for the Number Ten, but it didn't look like it was ever gonna come.

I hate takin' the bus. If I hadn't flunked driving school I'd be cruisin' to work every day. Cruisin' in Trax's uncle Eddie's car. Said I could use it for the summer. Said I just needed to pay for gas and make sure I took care of it.

Mr. Conrad. He had it in for me. I'm sure of it. Said I flunked the last test. Said I needed more work on my *driving* skills. Man, I could drive way better than anyone else in that stupid class. Mom says I got to wait until next spring to take the whole class over. That means I won't be able to even go for my license until *next* summer. I'll be seventeen by then. A seventeen-year-old, no-license-havin', no-date-gettin' loser.

No wheels.
No girls.
No sex.
No
life.

My ass is on fire

from the heat comin' off the engine. This bus is even hotter than our apartment. I told Mom we needed to fix the AC, but she said we didn't have the money for it. She says fans are just as good as AC. Fans? All fans do is blow around hot air. Makes the place feel like a sauna.

Mom thinks she knows *everything*.

I hate takin' the Twenty-eight

Stops everywhere. Every run-down neighborhood in Bandon.

I look out the window and watch the neighborhoods change, like different scenes in a movie. Broken glass and trash line the entrance to the bus stop.

Over by Lymon Avenue now. Gets a little shady over here. Lots of drugs, gangs, people up to no good. Mom doesn't like me takin' the Twenty-eight. Says one day I might get shot. Mom thinks everyone's gonna get shot.

Just as easy to get shot at the Gardens, so what's the difference? "Hospitals aren't as good over where the Twenty-eight stops," Mom says.

Just Another Brutha

I notice a couple of *hard*-lookin' kids getting on at Willis Street. They both are wearin' hoodies, with the hoods pulled over their heads. One in red, one in gray.

Gangstas for sure. I don't think they even feel the heat. They operate on some other current, they're in their own universe. Unaffected by *anything*.

All they know is *what* they know. Which is the streets, for real.

All I know is I'm not gonna look at them. These kids will bust a cap in you without even *thinkin'* about it.

The two gangstas start walking towards the back of the bus. *Not in front of me, not in front of me . . .*

They stop right in front of me. Like they knew what I was thinking. They're bigger than what I first thought. All muscle underneath their sweatshirts. They look older,

maybe seniors, older than that, even.
I can feel their eyes on me. I don't look up. I close my
eyes like I'm asleep. Shutting them tight, hopin' to God
they stop staring.

Come on, I'm just another brutha from the Heights, just like
you. I don't go to Graham, no way. I'm down, just like you.
Can't you tell?

"You got the time?" the gangsta in the gray hoodie
asks me. Prolly wants to see what kind of watch
I'm wearin'.

"Sorry, man, don't have a watch," I answer back, as polite
as I can without sounding like a punk. Keeping my left
hand in my pocket the whole time.

All a part of the game. All a part of the game.

Straight-up Gangstas

Just my luck. I have to be on the bus with these thugs. A
couple of Heights kids, for sure. Cromwell Heights, the
'hood to end all 'hoods. Starts at Willis Street and goes on
as far as it wants to. . . . The Heights got like the highest
crime rate in all of Florida. People get shot there every
night, twice on Sundays.

The gangsta with the red hoodie is staring at my face.

Probably thinks I'm a little *too* light. He's got that skeptical look. I see that look on the bus all the time. Out here, in the 'hood, they don't know biracial exists. All they know is that I'm a little too light to be black . . . and I don't speak Spanish, either. So they check off that "other" box in their head. "Other" means you *ain't* a brutha. So you ain't down.

That can be a dangerous thing around here.
Real dangerous.

I go to Graham

and that's about the worst place you can go to around here. See, Graham is all white. Except for me and Hank Carter. But he's on the basketball team. That's not like being a regular person. All sports stars get special treatment at Graham. It's like regular society doesn't apply to Carter, just as long as he gets his twenty points and ten rebounds, of course.

See, Bandon is like split in two:
There's the white section—the haves.
And the black section—the never had shit.

Truth be told, most of the "haves" don't even live in Bandon. They live in Milburn, which is right next to Bandon. That's where Graham is. You'd think it was a different country, as nice as it is over there. Everyone livin' behind gates, and right on golf courses.

It's off the chain.

The rest of the regular white folks live in Bandon.
They're mostly just like the rest of us, except they were
able to move a few blocks east. Not much difference, if
you ask me. Where I live, in Sunny Gardens, that's like
right on the border. Like Checkpoint Charlie or
somethin'. We got whites and blacks and everything in
between. But everyone's got one thing in common:
everyone's got

nothin'.

I feel one of the gangstas move closer to me
his leg almost touching my knee.

*Man, I hope they're not gonna start somethin'. That would be
all I need today.*

These kids, they definitely don't go to Graham. I don't
know where they go. All I know is that they hate kids
from Graham. Everybody from the Heights hates Graham
Crackers. That's what they call us. They think we're all
privileged kids with money. Wouldn't matter if I schooled
them on who I was, what I was. How I didn't *have* nothin',
never had nothin', and probably never *will* have nothin'.
Wouldn't change a thing. They'd still want to kick my ass.

Or worse.

Only reason I got into Graham was because of Trina

Mom's friend Trina, who she doesn't really talk to anymore, put me up for one of those minority scholarships. Then the craziest thing happened—I got the scholarship. Guess Graham thought I'd be good company for Hank Carter.

Man, they work fast when they want you. I was all set by the time last fall came around. Just in time to start my sophomore year. Trina bought my books, uniform, and paid for what the scholarship didn't cover for tuition. Mom says Trina don't make much more than she does. But ever since I can remember, Trina's hooked me up. I would never say it to Mom, but I know if it wasn't for Trina, my birthdays would've sucked, for real. I know Trina sent me stuff that Mom said *she* got me. I know it, 'cause I know my mom. And I know she don't like spendin' money, for real.

Trina's been kinda like my fairy godmother. Too bad I only got to meet her once, 'cause the way Mom talks about her sometimes, I doubt I'll ever get to see her again.

I can't believe this

I look down at my backpack lying proudly on the grimy bus floor. I stare at the letters almost shouting up at me.

The gangsta kids are staring at them, too. Three sets of
eyes fixed on two words: GRAHAM PANTHERS.

So this is how it's gonna start

Two more stops. Hurry up.

The gangstas are sizing me up, wondering if they can take
me easy, or if I'll put up a fight. Asking me the time was
just the first step. If they think they can take me, they'll
try somethin' the first chance they get.

I quickly take my eyes off my backpack and stare straight
ahead, acting as calm as I can. I got a little size to me, just
enough to *maybe* make them think I wouldn't be a
pushover. I puff out my chest and put on my meanest
glare. My constipated pissed-off look. It usually works. I
hope it works on *these* kids.

The bus lurches forward and stops too quick, almost
hitting an old lady standing at the bus stop. The gangsta
with the gray hoodie almost falls into my lap. He looks at
his buddy, who's laughin' at him. Then he looks at me, his
eyes small slits of hate, stabbing me with their glare.

He gets back on his feet, quick. "What's your problem,
punk?"

Now the gangsta in the red hoodie is all up in my face.

Both of them getting louder, angrier by the second. The gangsta in the gray hoodie puts his hand in his waistband. "I said, what's your problem, *punk?*"

So this is how it's gonna start.

I don't wait around any longer. Almost in one motion—I grab my backpack, leap past the gangstas, and fly out the back door of the bus. I'm still one stop away from work, but I don't care.

That might not have had a happy ending. I'm already covered in sweat, and my throat feels like I just swallowed a bucket of sand. I glance at my watch—ten fifteen. I'm gonna get fired for sure.

CHAPTER THREE

Lot Boy

"Jay, you should've called, man. Bennett is mad as hell. I'd steer clear of him if I were you." Trax is wiping down the wheels of a Rainmaker 7860 and getting on my case at the same time. "Yo, pass me the tire gloss."

I hand Trax the gloss and he starts squirtin' like there's no tomorrow. "Trax, you take this job way too serious. Man, why don't you slow down? You gonna be done with the whole fleet before lunch, then what are we gonna do?"

"Hey, lot boy, get over here." Mr. Bennett's voice is half rasp, half slime. What you would call a *very* slick dude. And that's not a compliment.

Bennett comes closer, but not too close. Acting like he might catch somethin' from me if he does. He points in the direction of his office, staring at me as I'm crouching on one knee, scraping off some dog shit from the rear passenger tire of the Rainmaker.

Lot boy. I hate that name. *Just another way to keep us down.* See, I'd take that as a racial slur if he didn't call Trax that, too. But he doesn't care what you are. He's an equal-opportunity asshole.

Bottomless Pits

Bennett, he's one of those bosses who loves the power. That's his drug. I guess he gets off on putting down high school kids. *Big man, real big man.* Now he's got everyone here callin' us lot boys.

Bennett, he's got a *serious* racket going. Gets these big campers for next to nothin', fixes them up, gets us to clean them for next to nothin', then turns them around and sells them at almost brand-new prices. I don't know how he does it, but people do buy these things. Soon as he gets one, it's practically sold.

Where do folks get the money to fill up these bottomless pits?

"I'll be right there." I have to shout over the loud drilling sounds coming from the garage.

"You better kiss his ass if you want to keep this job."

27

Trax is sounding like my mom all of a sudden.

"I ain't kissin' nobody's ass." I get up, knees crackin' as I walk over to his office.

God, I hate this job.

Jekyll and Hide

The smell of grease and sweat almost makes me gag as I walk through the garage, past the mechanics and some other low-budget workers.

I wonder what they pay these guys. Probably nothin', just like me.

I walk past Jekyll and Hide. Real names are Jonas and Johnson. Me and Trax call 'em Jekyll and Hide 'cause *Jekyll* (Jonas) will just go off on you for no reason, then the next second he'll be all nice and stuff. And *Hide* (Johnson), well, when he goes off, you just better hide.

Definitely two of the biggest and meanest-lookin' dudes I've ever seen. They scare the shit out of me, for real. They look like those big-ass professional wrestlers who fight in those fake matches. But with *these* dudes I *know* it ain't gonna be fake. It's gonna be *your ass.*

Jekyll is carrying some big-ass RV part, and Hide is trying to rip something out of an engine. They look at me like everybody here looks at me. Like a *lot boy*. A second-class citizen.

"Hey, lot boy, hand me that Phillips," Hide barks at me, not even looking up from the engine.

I look down on the oily cement floor next to where he's working. There's like sixteen different tools lying there: wrenches, screwdrivers, all kinds of stuff. I know what a Phillips is, but right now I panic. Somethin' in Hide's voice is tellin' me not to screw up or it's *my ass*. I pick up a regular screwdriver and hand it to him.

"This ain't no Phillips, lot boy."

"Damn, you dumb as you look." Jekyll starts laughing.

Everyone in the garage stops what they're doing and looks at me. Laughing and staring at the lot boy who doesn't even know what a stupid Phillips screwdriver is.

"Sorry, man." I try to sound cool, but it comes out weak, as usual.

Slick and Fake
I walk past the laughter and hard stares of the garage, into the showroom.

Past the almost new-lookin' RVs and campers, there's a family with two little kids looking at a Road Warrior. The salesman is tellin' them what they want to hear. That's Conaway, one of the more slimy salesman here at Bennett's RV and Camper Outlet. He'd prolly sell his own mother if he could get a decent price.

"Porter, get in here." Mr. Bennett sounds mad. He waves his hand at me to come into his office. Mr. Bennett's office looks just like him. Slick and fake.

He's got a shelf with a bunch of trophies on it. All different kinds of sports. Trax says he gets them made for him so it looks like he's won tournaments and stuff. It smells like axle grease and real bad cologne in here, too. Like that perfume they try to spray on you as you're walkin' into the SaveMart. Bennett's desk has a stack of papers on it that look like they've never been touched. Just window dressing. Just like him.

Bennett sits right across from me, head down, shuffling and reshuffling his papers. Now he gets up and passes right by me to get a cup of coffee. Completely ignoring me.

He sits back down and takes a long slimy slurp from his coffee mug, taking what seems like hours before he speaks. He doesn't look at me. Not once.

"I know you need this job. You need *me* a hell of a lot more than I need *you*. So I suggest you start making a better effort to get here on time. In case you don't get that hint, what I'm saying is: if you're late one more time, you're fired. Understand, amigo? *Comprende?*"

"Yeah, I understand," I say, without looking at him.

"Good, now get back to work. I don't have any more time to waste on lot boys today. I'm trying to run a business here, in case you haven't noticed."

Trax can't buy a break

"What he say?" Trax asks, his mouth full of peanut-butter sandwich. Lookin' like a poor man's Eminem, with his long, white-hot Miami Heat jersey—almost to his knees—and a red Yankees cap cocked to one side.

"You know, just the man tryin' to keep me down. Hey, wait a minute—you're the man, too." I try to get Trax to laugh, but he's not in the mood at all.

"Come on, Jay, this is serious, man. What he say?"

"You know, just being his usual slimy bustah-self. Told me next time I was late, he'd fire me. I hate that dude, definitely don't trust him. I don't trust anyone doesn't look you in the eye when he talks to you."

"Trust ain't got nothin' to do with it. He's the boss, and he can fire your ass. You got to stay on top of things, Jay. It's gonna look bad on me, too, you know. I'm the one who got you in, remember?"

I can hear the worry in his voice, plain as day. I know he needs this job more than me. He's got a little boy to think about. I can't imagine havin' a kid—bein' sixteen and in high school. Well, he doesn't have to worry about the high school part; he dropped out last year. That's why he takes this job so serious.

Damn, Trax can't buy a break. Right when he thought things were getting better, his girlfriend left him. Fine honey, nineteen, too. Trax had it made. He was stayin' with her in a real nice crib not far from Graham. He said she was an exotic dancer. I told him that's just a fancy name for a stripper. Whatever you want to call her, she's a cold bitch, *for real*. She took little Tyler and won't even let Trax see him. Now Trax is back at Sunny Gardens, livin' with his mom.

Trax's mom makes my mom look like a Sunday school teacher, for real. She's *always* out. I've been to his apartment like a million times, I only seen her *once*. I don't know what she does, don't wanna know either. I don't know how he makes it. Maybe he gets paid a little more than me, but not much. Probably gets some government help, too. I hope so.

It'll be cool
Don't worry
I'm not gonna mess up anymore
The heat's taken all the fight out of me, and its only
twelve fifteen. Must be ninety-five, *easy*. There's no way I
can tell Trax I have to start summer school in two weeks.
He'd freak, for sure. I know Bennett would rather fire me
than take me at part-time. I should just quit—this job
sucks anyway—but I need the cash. Mom's been messin'
up a lot lately. One mistake and that's *it*. She's liable to get
fired any day, with how she's been carryin' on. I don't
know if I'd trust her with *my* medical records. She says
she just puts stuff in the computer all day. But still, one
mistake and that's the end of that.

"Sorry to get on you so much, Jay. It's just, well, you
know, I don't want to see you get fired, and I just can't
afford any—"

"It's cool, Trax. Don't worry. It's gonna work out. It will."

Outside Game
I've worked on that for a long time. That outside game.
The one I show most people. How it looks like I'm
positive all the time. Things will work out, stuff like that.
Things prolly won't work out, that's what I should've
told Trax. I should have said that he's gonna be at this
dead-end job for the rest of his pathetic life, and not only

will it not work out, but it's gonna get even worse. Much worse. That's what I should've said, if I really wanted to help the brutha out with some truth. Give him the heads-up on the rest of his life. But I don't want to crush his spirit. He's got it hard enough as it is.

I finish off the rest of my fruit punch and take one last gulp of cool air before I go back to the lot. I see one of the garage dudes drive out a big-ass Sky-Way into spot fifteen.

"Looks like that one has our name on it." Trax actually sounds excited, like he can't wait to get out there and start workin' in that microwave on wheels.

"Trax, man, I'll prolly lose ten pounds in sweat today, *easy.*"

CHAPTER FOUR

MC Pretty

I can see it.
All I need is two turntables and a microphone . . . be a rap star,
for real. Now, if I could only rap . . .

I stare into the mirror, krumpin' for the cameras. I got
that good skin. Layla says it's like cocoa butter.

SAH-moooth.

My hair is like half'n'half, though. I can see the white
and black plain as day. *Mom and Dad.* More kinked-up
curly in the back, straighter in the front. Then it's kind
of a combo thing in the middle. Makes it real hard to
control when it's long. That's why I try to keep it
short.

I let myself air-dry from my shower, trying to keep the cold water on my skin for as long as possible. No towel needed when your apartment is like living on the sun.

Swimming on the Couch

I hear the shouting followed by the sound of breaking glass.

That would be the Hugheses next door. Goin' at it again. You can set your clock by them.

I turn up the volume on the TV and sit down on the couch. I got on the least amount of clothes possible. Just a bathing suit. That's it. I wouldn't wear anything, if it wasn't for the fact that Mom might come rollin' in at any time.

Yeah, she says don't wait up, but sometimes she comes home early. Mostly when she's had a bad day. Mom can even have a bad day on Saturday, so I'm always on my guard. You never know when she'll want to come home and take it out on me.

I hate those days.
Hate the nights worse.

The shouting gets a little louder

I crank up the TV as loud as it will go. Nothin' on, as

usual. Can't get anything anyway. I told Mom we have to have cable to get any kind of decent reception in this building, but she answered me the same as always. "No money for it. Too bad."

No money, yeah right. She's got enough money to go to the bar and drink all night.

She's such a hypocrite.
Such a liar.
Just a drunk.

The Slide

Time feels like it's going fast. I just sit on the couch, trying to keep out all the bad thoughts.
Trying to keep it all out.

I feel myself starting to slide. That familiar sinking feeling in the pit of my stomach that tells me my outside game is starting to crack. I feel real nervous, anxious, too. Like somethin' bad's gonna happen any second.

I look at the clock: one fifteen.

I've been sitting on this couch all night. Only got up to go to the bathroom and make a sandwich. Mom's right, I don't sleep. It's so hard to rest when everything in your head is wrong and you don't know how to make it right.

I am sliding deeper. But I know the slide will stop as soon as . . .

I open the door

and step out onto the breezeway—the outdoor corridor that leads to the bank of elevators on the right, and the south wing on the left. The Gardens is just like those old-folks buildings they have in Boca. All outside hallways leading to apartments and elevators.

Here, on eighteen, we're only two floors from the top. It can get a little dicey when the breezeway's packed after work, kids bouncin' around. Makes it hard to walk. This place used to be all old folks, too, until it got too crazy for them. Too many crazy moms and their kids actin' the fool. Must have got all their blood pressures up.

I walk closer to it now. Closer to the rail.

Just three rungs. Just three pieces of metal.

That's all that separates us.

I smile to myself. Why am I smiling? I feel guilty for what I want to do, but I know it will end this pain that I feel.

I know *I* can end it. Anytime I want.

The First Time

It's so much cooler outside. Little breeze, too, *feels nice.* I
step right to the rail and look down.

Eighteen floors of night, straight down. Night,
forever.

My heart starts beating faster. I feel excited and scared
at the same time. I drift off into the one memory
that always comes, the one that comes when I'm
close to the rail. The first time, the first time I can
remember . . .

I am small, walking with Mom, pushing the cart. Aisles as tall
as trees. Big cereal boxes stacked high like LEGOs. The smell of
popcorn and fresh-baked doughnuts makes me hungry. A lady is
giving samples of cheese stuck on little toothpicks. The toothpicks
remind me of little skinny people. Little skinny people stuck into
pieces of cheese . . . I am nagging Mom about wanting some
candy. She says no, like always. I reach for my favorite candy
bar: $20,000 Fudge.

The next thing I know, I am staring up at Mom. Screaming
and crying. My face hot like a fire was burning on it. My
leg hurts too. I can taste blood on my tongue. Mom's half-
closed hand hitting me so fast, I can't even believe it was
her. It was like I was knocked down by something I couldn't
even see.

39

People are starting to gather, staring down at me, whispering,
shaking their heads, pointing fingers. My arm feels like it's being
ripped out of its socket, as Mom practically lifts me up off the
ground and out of the store. Carrying me by that one arm all
the way to the bus stop. All the way. I am still crying, scared and
mad. Not at Mom, at myself. I must have done something
wrong, but I don't know what it was.

"It's all your fault, you shouldn't have made me do that to you."

That's all she says. Not a word more. Never says she's sorry, or
asks if I'm alright. Nothing.

At home that night, Mom shuts her door and goes to bed. I cry
myself to sleep. This becomes routine. This becomes my life.

I lean against the rail
The warm cheap steel feels good
against my bare skin.
I push harder.
This is all that separates me. . . .
Looking out into this nowhere land I live in,
there is not a drop of water in sight.
What's the use of living in Florida if there's no ocean?
Nothin' here but dead-end streets
leading to all-you-can-buy buffet strip malls,
leading back to nowhere.
I rub the rail with my left hand,

tightening my grip with my right.

I stare down into the black.

Into the end, or is it the beginning?

Now I feel most of my weight against the rail—

pushing even harder, pushing . . .

It feels good to push.

It feels good to get so close.

Getting closer every time.

I watch an old Camaro peel out of the back parking lot,

the screeching tires breaking my trance.

I step back from the rail.

Stepping slowly back,

onto the breezeway.

Sunday Morning

I feel myself start to wake up before my eyes are open.

The heat makes my skin itch. I try to turn over in

bed, but there's no escape. Hot everywhere. Nothin'

but hot.

Sunday morning. Some moms get up and cook a nice

Sunday breakfast. Eggs, bacon, toast—never happens

around here. Mom's sleeping one off, for sure. She tried

to sneak in about four, but I heard her. Knocking over

the kangaroo clock on the table by the front door.

Slamming her bedroom door, like she's the only one who

lives here.

I get out of bed in one motion. I'm already sweating as I walk into the kitchen and open the freezer door. I stick my head in, *feels so good*. I take the ice tray out and set it on the end table next to the couch. That should last me the morning. Prolly holds like two pounds of ice in that thing. It's not really a tray, more like a portable ice maker. One of those *big* ice containers that's supposed to stay in the freezer. The *hell* with that, I got to have the freezer come to me today. Too hot to be goin' back and forth all day.

The cold ice feels good on my chest. Two big handfuls of cubes are quickly melting. Rivers of cold water are collecting in my belly button. I am almost cool, almost.

"This ain't no country club"

"Get your big feet off that coffee table. I paid good money for that thing. I don't want your smelly feet stinkin' it up. You better not drip any water on the carpet, either."

Mom. I didn't hear her get up. She comes wobbling out of her bedroom in mid yell. Like she woke up yelling. Maybe she did. Her face is all scrunched up tight, her eyes are squinty-looking, like it's painful for her to keep them open. Looking at her now it's hard to imagine she was *ever* a model, but that was a long time ago, a *long* time ago.

Mom looks kind of beat up, not by fists, but by years. The way she's lived her years. Lines and marks, puffy patches of hard times and late nights permanently dot her face. Her long blonde hair is pulled up into a wild-looking ball, sitting on top of her head. Her robe half open. Mom was never inhibited. She doesn't care what people see, even me. She's a *mess*.

She walks towards me like she's on a mission. As she gets close, I start getting that feeling again. The one that tells me Mom is not doing too well this morning. The one that is warning me to be careful.

"It's just water, it's not gonna hurt nothin'." I know as soon as the words leave my mouth, I shouldn't have said them. Not on *this* morning.

"Don't talk back to me, Jayson"

"I will put you out in a second. Don't forget who pays for this place. Pays for all your food, your clothes, too. You think that little part-time job's gonna make ends meet? I'd like to see you make it out on those streets by yourself. You'd get eaten alive. So watch your mouth, if you know what's good for you."

Mom grabs the container of ice cubes off the end table and stumbles into the kitchen, spilling half of them on her way in. She's tall for a woman, probably close to five eleven. She looks even taller when she's mad. Stretching her neck, lifting her chin like she was a bird or somethin'. *Like a vulture* . . .

"This place is a mess. Didn't I tell you to clean it up? I think I did. Do you like making me mad? Is that it, Jayson? You do, don't you? I would have thought you'd learned your lesson. Where the hell are those cookies I bought yesterday? Did you eat them all? You stupid little—"

First
I hear the crash of
ice and plastic
and
skin
all coming together in
an instant,
like a lightning strike hitting
a tree.

Then
I feel the sting,
followed
by the knifing pain
caused by the ice container
making contact with the back of my head.

Now

Mom reloads and hits me again before I have a chance to protect myself. More ice cubes are falling everywhere, some of them spilling out and landing on top of me. I fall forward and grab my head with both hands, waiting for the next blow. I know she's just warming up. I close my eyes, gripping my head, curling into the fetal position on the couch. My hands feel wet.
Is that water
or
blood?

I wait. Don't want to move. Don't want to give her any more reason to get *really* crazy. I wait some more.

But the next blow doesn't come. Mom is halfway to her bedroom by the time I raise my head. I hear the door slam, then the sound of a man's voice.

That's why. She's got somebody in there.

I get up fast and grab my wallet and house keys

I throw on a T-shirt and head out the door. *I should just do it now, get it over with, once and for—*
I stop at the rail. I run my hands over it. The chipped black paint is as hot as a frying pan. I let my hands get

45

hot. It hurts, but it feels good, too. I lean over, letting my
head dangle out into the close, thick air. Letting the hot
wind soothe my mother's touch.

I look straight down. My stomach flutters, I get that
weird feeling down below. Not like when you're with a
girl. But more like when you think you're gonna die.
Like when you're flying around a curve on a coaster and
you think for a second you might fly off the track.
Yeah, like that.

I lean over the rail, *sliding deeper and deeper into myself* . . .
I wish I could just make it stop. Tear out the pain with
my fingernails, but I can't get to it. It feels like battery
acid, eating me alive from the inside out.

I step up off the breezeway landing and onto the
first rung of the rail. I lean over some more. Looking
straight down. The feeling getting stronger . . .
stronger . . .

I'm gonna do it this time, I'm really gonna do it. . . .

I hear a lock turn and the sound of a door starting to
open. I jump down off the rail, back onto the
breezeway, and head for the stairs. Running down flights
as fast as I can. It's so hot I can barely breathe in the
stairwell. I start coughing, the sweat pouring down my

face. I stop at *seven* and push open the stairway door. I hope he's home.

I really hope he's home.

CHAPTER FIVE

A Human Vomit Hose

"What the—?"

The unguided missle of vomit hits Trax square in the chest. I am now the human vomit hose. The super-puke hero I become when Mom is having a "bad" day. Puke flies out of my mouth, backing Trax into his living room, causin' him to trip over the coffee table and lose his balance. I am sure that food from *kindergarten* is splattering onto the floor. I feel like I'm out of my body, but I can still feel the pain.

Sweat and

tryin' to catch my breath. Finally the dry heaves arrive, like an old friend you haven't seen in years. So glad they're here . . . but after five minutes . . .you can't wait for them to leave.

Trax peeks around the couch and looks at me like he
wants to wave a white flag. I just collapse onto the floor.
Holding the back of my head. Wishing I had done it.

Today.
The rail.
Wishing
I had the guts.

Just Another Afternoon . . .
TRAX:
Damn, they suck. They should just move that team out of
town, do us all a favor.

ME:
Look at that dude, he couldn't catch a cold. How do you
drop a ball like that? They need to trade his ass, and I
mean tomorrow. . . .

TRAX:
Yeah, he does suck, but the rest of the team really ain't
that bad. It's not like they don't have talent. I mean they
got some pretty decent players—

ME:
I think it's the manager, he just sucks donkey balls.

Me and Trax sitting in his living room, watchin' the

baseball game. Normal as can be. I just flip my switch, and it's like it never happened. Mom and the rail fade like some movie I can't remember very well. Innings go by like they always do. Nothin' special about this game or this day. *Nothin' special.* Trax is staring straight ahead, eyes on the game. I am reading his new T-shirt. The one *without* the puke:

HEY, YOU CHEAP BASTARD,
QUIT READING MY T-SHIRT
AND BUY YOUR OWN.

A smile tries to force its way across my face. But my switch got flipped back. Mom's angry face and the ice tray pop into my head and quickly erase my smile. I can feel each blow, just like she's hitting me again. . . . I can feel it. I can.

Insult to Injury

"How ya doin?" Trax doesn't look up from the game. I know he's not just askin' about how I feel. He wants to know what the hell happened to me today. But "How ya doin?" is about as close as he'll ever come to prying into my life.

I know he knows about my mom—not everything, just that she's got a temper. But most folks know that. Sometimes I wish I could tell Trax about the rail. I know

he wouldn't understand. He'd probably think I was crazy.
Maybe I am. . . .

"I'm cool," I answer. Everybody in that apartment including his cat, Furball, knows that was an out-and-
out lie.

"Cool." Trax says. Furball comes out of hiding just long
enough to scratch my hand as I try to pet him.
Insult to injury.

The knot on the back of my head

has been expanding with every inning, the ice pack
melting too fast to keep up with the swelling. Trax got
AC, but it's, like, so weak, it won't cool the place off until
December.

"Want some grub? Got some Sizzle Snacks, I think, like
Philly steak and cheese or somethin'." Trax looks up at
me, real sly-like. Like he doesn't want me to know that
he's looking at me. Doesn't want me to see the worry on
his face.

*I must be **all jacked up** if Trax is worried about me.*

"Not hungry," I answer as I swallow some more aspirin. I
can still taste the puke in my mouth. I feel myself getting
tired, wantin' to shut my eyes. . . . I push back into the

Barcalounger, making my final approach to sleep.

"Yo, Jay, don't go to sleep. You might have a concussion or somethin'. Man, I'm not havin' you go into a coma on me. I know you'd sue my ass for sure." Trax is half joking, but I know he's half serious too.

"How am I supposed to stay awake? Not like this game's got any action to it." I take the ice pack off and stare at the dried blood that's stuck to it. I rub the bump, which now feels like a small mountain.

Geeee-zus—she knocked the shit out of me this time.

Monsters

I am real small, and we're on the move. I am scared. Mom is screaming at some man, explaining something. Pleading with the man for something. He shakes his head and says no. Never looking at my mom, never looking at me . . . The man's face looks like Dracula, and he's got fangs. His skin is almost trans-parent. We are running, fast, away from Dracula. Actually, Mom is running, I am just being pulled along behind her. Like a little kid caboose. Being flung around curves and bends. Lifted over fire hydrants and broken sidewalk. Mom tells me to wait. People stare at us. We ride up a creaky elevator and walk down the hall. It smells like rotten eggs and pee. We have to step over weird-looking creatures with wings lying in the middle of the hallway. Mom opens the door and throws me on the bed. I am

watching TV and Mom is on the phone. She makes calls all
day. She talks on the phone, but never talks to me. Monsters
bang on the door, trying to get inside. Monsters everywhere,
always trying to get us. . . .

I should know better

"Yo, Jay, Jay . . . Jayson, what are you doin', man?" I look
up to see Trax's big broken-out face all up in mine. Like
lookin' at the moon on a big-screen TV.

"What, what happened?" I manage to stammer. I am not
awake enough yet to really feel the crazy-intense
pain that the bump on my head is giving me. I start to
remember bits and pieces of the dream. Monsters,
mostly.

I should know better by now, like Mom says. There really is
no escape, not even in my dreams.

Poor Trax

"You fell asleep, that's what happened. I thought maybe
you slipped away. Man, maybe I should take you to the
ER, get that thing looked at." Trax is pointing to the
giant-size knot on the back of my head, which is hurting
like hell again.

"No, I'll be alright." I get up off the Barcalounger and

walk slowly to the bathroom. I turn my head and look into the mirror. There it is, rising up like a volcano through a rain forest. DAMN.

I grab some more aspirin from the medicine cabinet and splash water on my face. Soaking a washcloth and squeezing the cool water onto the top of my head. Letting it run down my forehead, to my face—down to my waist, down my legs. Forming little rivers that flow in between my toes.

I open the bathroom door and walk back to the living room. Trax is in the kitchen, talking on the phone. He sounds stressed, like whoever he's talking to is squeezing the shit out of him with their words.

I walk into the kitchen, pretending like I'm looking for something in the refrigerator. Trax is pacing back and forth, keeping the phone glued to his ear like his life depends on it. Trax isn't saying much. He says the most with his expression: a crumpled-up look of hurt and pain, with some disbelief thrown in for good measure. I think he stole that look from *me*.

"It doesn't have to be this way," Trax finally says. He sounds desperate.

Prolly his girl. That's my cue. Time to roll.

I feel sorry for him, but I can't get involved. I got my own shit to deal with. I wave at Trax, and mouth to him to call me. He nods, but I can tell he is totally preoccupied with his listening and pacing.

Quarter till five

I walk out of Trax's place and onto the breezeway. It smells like Mom's fingernail polish remover and nasty Bandon funk. There is a steady stream of people going in and out next door. Trax's neighbors are known druggies. *Man, don't they ever work?*

I can't tell if the elevator smells like puke or I do. Probably both. It opens at the first floor, but only three-quarters of the way. *That's the Gardens for you. Nothin' ever works a hundred percent.*

The sun is still blazin', even though it's late afternoon. I glance at my watch. Quarter till five. Gotta stay out at least until eight, then hope that Mom stays over at Lonnie's house again. She usually stays with him on Sundays. Mom says that's their day of rest. Yeah, right. Lonnie's the one she's been on-again, off-again with. Not the dude she was with this morning. I don't know who he was. Never saw his face. Heard his voice, but it didn't sound like Lonnie. Lonnie is a shady dude (and that's an understatement). That's all Mom likes. Them bad-boy types. That's why she's always gettin' dumped.

55

Man, I hope she stays at Lonnie's tonight.

I walk down Gilliam

and cut across Nobly. Through the vacant lot they keep
sayin' they're gonna build another complex on. That's all
we need around here, *another* Sunny Gardens.

I'm not sure where I'm headed, but anyplace is better
than goin' back home. Maybe I'll go to The Grinds, get
an iced coffee. The thought starts to cool me down, and
calm me, too.

War Zone

I guess I needed to see him. Wanted to see him. Even
though it's never good for me
to see him.

I swallow the last of my iced-caramel whatever the hell it's
called and walk to the front entrance. Dad lives two streets
over from The Grinds. Two streets and two worlds away.

Brick walkways turn into broken sidewalks and burned-
out buildings. A war zone, for real. Button-down business
men out with their kids become crack zombies, beggin'
for money. Even cops don't stop in this neighborhood.

5C

Dad's building looks like a prison. Mesh wire and bars on

most of the windows. *Who are they afraid of? All the criminals live inside.*

A guard stands out front, tryin' to look tough. He doesn't even look at me. *Prolly just some dope fiend they put a uniform on.* The sign on the front lawn reads: ROBERT DORIAN HOUSES. Guess he was some rich white dude who funded this place. That's what Dad says, anyway. Now it's just another government project that's rotting away.

The front door is open to the entryway. Hot humid air and thick rotten funk hit me hard—I feel like I need an oxygen mask just to breathe. The smell makes me gag. Like someone took a dump right here.

Buzzers line the wall, in rows. I look for Dad's. 5C. I hold my nose and press the buzzer. Sacrificing my air to keep from puking *again*. Dad doesn't answer. I press the buzzer one more time and wait.

What the hell am I doing here?

High

"Hey, boy, what you doin' in the 'hood? Your moms finally kick you out?" Dad's usual greeting.

He looks worse. Didn't even know that was possible. He's

wearin' shorts with no shirt on. I can see his ribs, plain as day. His legs look like little kid legs. Skinny and small. His arms have no muscle tone at all. Black-and-blue bumps and scar tissue make them look almost deformed. Dad's dope life on display for *everyone* to see . . .

Dad is high. Which is a good thing, 'cause when he's fiending? Tryin' to get a fix? It's like starin' at the devil himself. His eyes cold and empty. Lookin' right through you like a desperate animal searchin' for his prey.

This was a mistake
I know it as soon as I see him. What is this junkie gonna do for me? He can't even help himself.

"Wanna drink? You old enough now. Gotta cold beer. Make you grow big and strong."

"No thanks." My skin starts to itch. Can't tell if it's 'cause I'm hot and sweaty or 'cause Dad's place is crawlin' with fleas and God knows what else. Dad's mangy dog, Killer, is lying by the fan in the corner of the living room. Letting the air blow onto his face. He doesn't even notice me. *He's prolly high too.* . . .

"Whatcha doin' here anyway, boy? Ringin' my buzzer like you was on fire or somethin'. You get mixed up in somethin'? Told you them streets would get ya sooner or

later." Dad's eyes start to roll back into his head, smiling at
the air. Some dope fantasy that only he can see. He shifts
his weight on the couch then settles back onto one of
the ripped cushions.

"No, I'm cool. Didn't get mixed up in nothin'. Just
thought I'd stop by." So used to tellin'everybody I'm
okay, it just flows out of my mouth, like it *was* the truth.

"Just checkin' . . . makin' sure you didn't get mixed up
with that bad element out there. Just makin' sure . . ."
Dad smiles at the air again—eyes closed. His head snaps
forward, then jerks up, like some invisible string is controlling him.

My dad, the marionette doll.

His eyes pop open—wide, like someone just shined a
light in them. He stares hard. Tryin' to figure out who I
am. Or tryin' to figure out what he can get from me.
Prolly needs money. He *always* needs money.

My head is hurting again

"You okay, boy? Don't look too good."

Even my dope-fiend dad can tell somethin's wrong.
Bet he can see it, too. I try to keep him from seeing the
back of my head. *Maybe he won't notice.*

I make up a lie—quick. "I'm cool, I gotta go. Gotta meet a friend."

"Whatcha come here for anyway . . . in the first place . . . if ya just . . .

gonna . . .

take off . . .

all . . .

sudden . . ."

Dad trails off. His eyes shut again. Slumped over to one side, but still sittin' up. Mouth half open.
Breathing heavy.

Breathing.

For now.

CHAPTER SIX

I keep walking
It's the only thing I can do.
I don't have the luxury of staying in bed.
Being depressed.
Havin' someone take care of me,
help me.

I'm alone.
Always been that way.
Always will be.
So,
I keep walkin'
as far as I can from
the Dorian Houses,
from
Dad and his dope.
From the crack zombies—
the walking dead.

I keep walking, but I know
I'll never *really* get away.

I am sinking deep

Like the sun's tryin' to do right now. I look down at my
feet, tryin' to take me back home.

*So tired, just want to lie down . . . don't care if I do slip into a
coma. . . .*

My skin starts itchin' again. *Dad's fleas.* It's unbearable.
The way I feel. I start to scratch at my skin. Scratching
until I feel the wet on my fingertips. Blood from the itch
that never goes away.

Ain't no fleas. It's my disease. My life. Maybe I should just
get a gun. Forget about the rail. But too much can go
wrong with that. End up livin' with half my head blown
off. *I've seen it before, on TV.*

No, jumpin' is the best way. I've done my research. It's
quick and easy. No pain. You pass out on the way down
anyway. Just a few seconds and its over.
Forever.

Everything is all lit up

Like someone just plugged in the city. Bandon at night
is nothin', really. Same as day, but a hell of a lot more

dangerous. I start to move a little faster. Even though I'm far from Dad's, I'm still not in a good area. 'Cause there are no good areas at night.

At night, anything can happen, anywhere, anytime. Actually, there are no *real* good areas *anytime* in Bandon. Even the white part of Bandon got it's bad parts. Truth be told, some of the white parts of Bandon are even more violent than the black parts. They just don't report it on the news. But if you live here, you know.

Almost Nine

And I just want to forget this day. Forget it ever happened. I walk up the front steps and into the lobby of my *palace*. Crazy Mrs. Diebold is talkin' to herself again. She sees me and tries to play it off like we've been havin' a conversation.

"Did you see that on the news, Jayson? They're comin' right up from Mexico. Those terrorists. Gonna try to blow us up again. You know Bandon is on their list. Saw that on the news, too. . . . I'm glad we're putting troops on the border. Shouldn't be sneaking into our country anyway. Too many foreigners here as it is. You know it's gonna be over a hundred tomorrow. Gonna be a hot one. . . . Heard they're gonna try to attack us from space. Those terrorists, you know, they can get up in space if they want to. Saw that on the news, too. . . ."

I don't even stop. Usually I'll just listen for a minute or two, just to be nice. But right now I could care less about that crazy old woman. Talkin' all her crazy paranoid stuff. Man, I wish they would blow up Bandon. Do us all a favor, for real.

I call the home phone, just one more time to make sure that she's gone. Tried a little while ago and no one answered. "Hello, you have reached . . ." Got the machine again. Must be over at Lonnie's. Thank God.

As soon as I turn the lock
I know.

She's home.

All the lights are on, and I hear music. The fear starts building up inside of me. I want to run. But where would I go? I rub the back of my head. It still aches, but I'll survive.

I open the door slowly and stick my head in first, never knowing for sure what I might be walking into. I take a quick look at the rail before I shut the door. *I feel better now. . . .*

"Hey, baby"

"Where you been? Me and Lonnie's about to fix us some popcorn. Want some?" Mom is hangin' on to one of Lonnie's gigantic arms. She looks like a long skinny white coat, and Lonnie's a big black hanger.

Lonnie just smiles his shit-eating grin. The one that says, *Look at me, I got me a fine white woman and she doesn't know that she's just one of many.*

Both of them are drunk. And happy, for the moment. They must be gettin' along, for the time being, anyway. Man, Mom is the *real* Jekyll and Hyde. *Hey, baby?* Doesn't she remember that she knocked the shit out of me this morning?

I walk straight to my bedroom

flop down on my bed and close my eyes. No luck. Not tired. I get up and sit down at my desk. Looking over papers, magazines, and mail that is still in the same spot it was days ago.

One envelope catches my eye. I pick it up and look closer. No return address. I tear it open to find a bright yellow card with two giant stereo speakers on the front. When you open the card, there's a hip-hop-lookin' kid with shades on and he's plastered to the wall. His hair's standin' straight up and his face looks like he just flew

65

upside down in one of those fighter jets. The card says,
IT'S NEVER LOUD ENOUGH!

I look down and quickly read the words that are written
there:

Hey Jay,
    What's up? I know this card is kinda corny but
it's all I could find. I have been thinking about you
and your mom, so I finally decided enough was enough
and it was time for me to put pen to paper! (Or in
this case, pen to card!) I wanted to tell you that it
was so great to finally meet you. You really seem
like a wonderful young man. I know it's been almost
a year now and I am so sorry that I haven't
written or been back to visit. (You know how life
gets in the way. . . .) I hope circumstances will
change and I'll be able to visit again sometime soon!
    I hope your liking you're new school, and every-
thing is going well with you and your mom. Below is
my mailing address. Please write me back and tell me
how your doing.

Take care.
Lots of love,
Trina

Last August
That was the first time I ever met her. Just saw her for

one day. I remember we all got ice cream, then we went to Graham to sign me up for classes. Trina said she was comin' back the next day to hang out some more, but when the next day came, Trina was gone.

Trina Jones and Mom

Best friends, from back in the day. Both of them tall, blonde, and strong Appalachian mountain women from Goner, West Virginia. You'd be a goner for sure if you stayed in that coal town. Had it rough when they were small. No money, food was scarce, too. Nothin' to look forward to but poverty and black lung, according to Mom. Got out as soon as they could. Both of them landing in New York City. Both of them with stars in their eyes . . .

Be nice if Trina and Mom would be friends again. I'd get to see her more. I'd get to see her *at all*.

Sick

"Oh, give it to me, Big Daddy. You're my big daddy . . ."

There should be a law against making a teenage boy listen to his mom and her boyfriend having sex all night. They should both be put in jail, and they should throw away the key. I have to go puke again.

The morning

doesn't come fast enough. I get up before Mom and
Lonnie. I ain't givin' her any chance to start some stuff
with me today. I throw on my clothes and head out the
door.

Don't have to be to work for an hour and a half. I feel
the heat already. Sun's barely up. I smile at my friend as I
walk to the elevators. Running my hands over it.
Stopping for a few seconds to grip the rail tight before
the elevator opens. Feeling relieved to be out of that
place.

Away from Mom.

Bennett's Office

"I don't know, Porter, you really are asking a lot of me.
It's bad enough you come in late half the time. Now you
want me to accommodate your summer-school schedule?
I'm gonna have to think about this one. Now get on out
to the lot. I'll give you my answer tomorrow. When did
you say you started school?"

"Next Monday, July fifth. A week from today." I try to
sound as official as I can.

Mr. Bennett nods me out the door and starts shuffling
papers. Back to his pretend work for the day. I should

have said more. Been more convincing. I really do need to keep this shitty job, not just for the money but to keep me away from *her*, at least for a few hours every day.

"Is he gonna let you work part-time?"
I want to tell him everything. I want to confess. Not about what Bennett said. But what I think about every day. How I want to jump off the rail and kill myself. I want to tell Trax everything I feel. Tell him what my mom does to me—what she's done . . . I want to tell him everything.

"Did he fire you, Jay? Jay?" Trax is startin' to get impatient. Sounding nervous. Prolly thinks I'm gonna mess it up for him if Bennett lets me go.

My urge to confess disappears as fast as it appeared. I'm not gonna tell him shit. He might go and try to do the right thing and report me to someone. Or worse, go and tell Mom.

No, I'm gonna keep my secret between me and the man upstairs. He understands what I want to do. I know God wouldn't want me to live with so much pain.

CHAPTER SEVEN

Under Attack

Pop, pop, pop, pop—pop-pop-pop

I jump out of bed and get on my hands and knees,
crawling on the floor towards my door. I still feel like I'm
asleep, but I'm on autopilot.

*Somebody is shooting at me. Shit, Mom finally went and
messed around with the wrong dude.*

I grab my baseball glove and put it on top of my head.
Like that's gonna stop a bullet.

I shut the door and lie facedown on the floor. Sweat is
starting to pool around my neck. I can feel it begin to
drip down my back. My heart feels like it's gonna
explode in my chest. *Who the hell is shooting—*

Pop, pop, pop—pop-pop-pop

I am lying flat on my stomach, both hands over my ears. *Man, I don't wanna go out like this. Not like this . . .*

Then it hits me. Not a bullet, but what day it is. *It's the Fourth.* Shooting guns in my neighborhood on the Fourth of July is like a tradition. Especially with these crazies at the Gardens. They got no sense. They don't even mess with fireworks, they go straight to the heavy artillery. Can't believe no one ever gets got, with all the shooting that goes on here. All them bullets goin' straight up in the air, they have to come down somewhere. Don't they?

Mom is gone

and that's cool by me. Don't even know if she came home last night. Don't care, either. Supposed to meet Trax later to watch some fireworks. Goin' over to Grisby Park. Only time I'll go over there is on the Fourth. Only time they got any cops patrolin' it. Otherwise that place is off-the-chain gangsta. The Wild West, for real. Wonder if Dad will be there. It's just a few blocks from his building. I don't wanna see him. Especially on the Fourth. He'll be wasted, for sure.

"Hey, cutie, what's up?"

Layla moves closer to me in the elevator. She smells like a mixture of beer, suntan lotion, and body odor.

Kinda like a funky piña colada. *Real sexy, Lay.*

"Where you off to? Got a hot date for the fireworks?"

"No, just goin' over to Grisby. Hang out with Trax."

"How come you ain't got no girlfriend? I know lots of girls who'd like to get with you."

I am praying for the elevator to move faster, but it just keeps its slow, jerking pace. *Wonder if the cable snapped and we went crashing down to the basement—if that would shut her up?*

"You really are turnin' into quite a handsome young man, Jay. You been workin' out?" Layla moves even closer. Her breath smells like rotten eggs and Listerine.

Okay, now she's *really* hitting on me. Layla Morrison's skanky ass is hitting on me in the elevator. She's the original "desperate housewife"—except this trick ain't got no house and she ain't nobody's wife, either.

Please, God, let the cable snap. Please . . .

Grisby Park
Wall-to-wall humanity. Everyone soaked with sweat, baby strollers chokin' up the makeshift grass aisles—which are the only way you can even get to an open spot. If you're

lucky enough to find one. Early evening and its still
ninety degrees.

"Humidity is what gets ya," Trax mumbles as we trip over
people and blankets, tryin' to find a spot to sit.

"This is the jam."

"Yeah it is." Me and Trax go into a spontaneous head
bounce as we get closer to the gigantic boom box sitting
on a checkered blanket, bags of chips and other snacks
surrounding it like fans to a rock star.

Me and Trax hurdle the blanket, barely clearing the boom
box. A brutha with dreads drinkin' a forty is bobbin' his
head to the beat and eyein' us to make sure we don't land
on his tunes. The smell of weed is so strong it makes my
eyes water.

"Man, errybody's here," I say, tryin' to sound like all those
West Coast rappers.

"Yeah they is." Trax is in full-on wiggah mode. Just get
him around a bunch of black folks and Trax becomes
blacker than everyone. Talkin' different, lookin' different. I
swear he gets two shades darker, for real.

Trax turns his hat all the way around and goes into a

gangsta lean as we stop for a minute and jam with the dreadlocks dude.

"Oh shit, Nelly's off the chain . . . 'Smile for me, Daddy . . .'" I start singin' along with Nelly and the dreadlocks dude.

"Yo Jay, there's a spot." All of a sudden Trax is airborne, diving headfirst into the tiniest piece of open real estate. "Home sweet, Jay, we home sweet, like a mug."

"You wanna hit, Jay?"
"Make ya forget all about your problems?"

Trax pulls out a joint from his pocket. "Sure need to forget about mine." Trax fires it up and takes a long hit. He starts coughin' and laughin' at the same time. "This is the chronic, Jay . . ."

"Man, I aint tryin' to catch a case 'cause you wanna forget your problems. You know how you get when you smoke. Always tryin' to start some shit."
"Come on, Jay, don't be such a drag. Take a hit. Come on. I'll be cool, I promise."

"I heard that before." I grab the joint from Trax's hand and take a big hit. I hold it as long as I can, blowin' out the smoke all in Trax's face.

I take another hit, then another. I feel everything start
to slow down. I start to feel lighter, forgetting all the
bad. . . . Slow motion gets even slower. . . . My eyes get
heavy.

I start trippin' on a little boy holdin' a red balloon,
dancin' on a blanket. He looks like a little windup toy . . .
I can almost see the key sticking out of his back. Man, I
should just reach over there and wind him up some
more. That shit would be *hi-larious*—

I try to refocus, but I can't. All of a sudden the little boy's
balloon turns into Mickey Mouse, except Mickey's got
dreads and he's drinkin' a forty. Okay, now I'm trippin'.
What the hell kind of weed was that?

OOOOOHHH and AAAAAAH

"Damn, when are they gonna start the show?"

"Oh shit, Jay, you must be high as hell. It's over.
Man, we gotta roll."

"What? Quit playin'."

"I ain't playin', man. You see all these people gettin' outta
here? It's over, Jay. You missed it."

"I must have passed out or somethin'."

"I tried to slow you down, but you were smokin' like it was the last weed on earth. Told you it would help you forget your problems."

"Didn't want to miss the whole fireworks, though. Man, what was in that weed? Did you let me smoke some loveboat, Trax? Did you? You did, didn't you? Man, I should—"

"Come on, Jay, lets bounce before it gets mad crazy up in here. Get up, Jay. GET UP!"

Beef

"Man, we'll never get on that bus. Let's walk." Trax is sounding impatient again. I hate when he gets like that.

"We are not walkin' on the Fourth of July all the way back to the Gardens—that's just askin' for trouble. Let's just wait, they'll be another."

People are pushing and shoving, trying to get on the bus. I step back off the curb, trying to get out of the crush. I can feel myself making contact with something other than the sidewalk. I know instantly what I did.

"Yo, man, did you just step on my LeBrons? You know these kicks cost more than your life. You want me to prove that to you?"

"Sorry, man, didn't mean to—"

"Yo, don't be disrespectin' my boy. I got his back." Trax stands in front of me, I try to push him away, but it's too late.

I knew this shit was gonna happen.

"You ain't got nobody's back, white boy. I will dust both of you."

Here we go.

"Come on, Trax, let's bounce, man. It's not worth it."

"You better listen to him, white boy, if you know what's good for you."

People are starting to clear out around us. That's the first sign that you know somethin' bad's about to happen. Nobody wants to get hit with a stray bullet.

"I ain't listenin' to nobody. And stop callin' me white boy, if you know what's good for *you.*"

"Trax!" I'm screamin' at him to stop. But Trax ain't listenin'. He's just standin' there, lookin' like some extra in a bad rap video. *Fuck.* Now he's gonna get us both killed.

77

For nothin'. Just gonna be a little blurb on the last page of the newspaper. Just a two-second mention on the evening news, right before they go to a commercial:

"Two teenage boys got smoked last night because one of them was a stupid white boy who got high and decided to start a beef with a brother from the 'hood."

"Well, Cindy, I suppose they deserved it."

"Yes indeed, Stu, I'm sure they did. Won't lose any sleep over those two."

"We'll be right back with some cooking tips you won't want to miss."

The first shot

whizzes over my head as people start screamin' and runnin' in all directions. For all his gangsta talk, Trax is halfway down the street before I can even yell out his name. Runnin' like a little girl, arms flailing at his sides. I take off down the street after Trax. Neither of us can go very fast, because about a thousand other folks are runnin' in the same direction—AWAY FROM THE SHOOTING.

Just another Fourth of July in Bandon, Florida. Can't wait till next year. . . .

The room is spinning

and I feel like there's a hundred little people with sledge-hammers goin' at it in my brain. I just finished drinkin' like a gallon of water and I'm still thirsty.

Mom's not home. So that's one good thing about tonight. Maybe Dad was right. Only a matter of time before them streets catch up to me.

I'm just glad that brutha was higher than us, 'cause if he was sober and could shoot straight? Me and Trax would be on the news right now, for real.

Kind of a trip how I want to snuff myself out, but I don't want anyone else doin' it for me. Guess I'm just selfish that way. Man, that's some shit you could write a paper on for school.

School. Just remembered the first day of summer school is tomorrow. That would've sucked, gettin' killed right before classes started. I bet Bennett would've gotten real mad at that.

"Goddammit, Porter, how could you get yourself killed right before school started, especially with me being so nice and letting you work part-time, so you could go. How could you be so dumb? Now get out on the lot. . . ."

Okay, I must still be high. I am gonna be *hurtin'* tomorrow, for real.

The sun is my alarm clock

Bright rays of heat slap my face and force me out of bed.
My head is pounding, I still feel dizzy, and I'm thirsty as
hell.

I stand in the shower, turning the handle all the way to
COLD. I let the *lukewarm* water run over my body,
loosening my muscles. *Feels like I was in a boxing match
last night.*

I fill up a couple of small plastic bottles with water and
ice, throw on my school clothes, and I'm out. I hate
wearin' these things. Black slacks and a white button-
down shirt that itches my neck. Blue blazer with the
letters JGDS surrounded by a gold crown, two old
fashioned-looking keys, and a shield with some jacked-up
writing on it.

"The Joseph Graham emblem, wear it proudly." That's
what Mrs. Longingham, the headmistress, said to me on
my first day of school last year—forcing a smile like
someone was holding a gun to her head. I'm sure she was
thinkin', *Not another one.*

I stare down at my feet. Black dress shoes (a size too small 'cause that's all that was left at SaveMart) are squeezin' the shit out of my toes. *God, I wish I could wear my Keds.* I look like a broke-ass Kanye West. Kind of preppy, but *my* clothes come from SaveMart, definitely not where Kanye shops.

I leave my shirt untucked to try and give it a *little* hip-hop flair, but it ain't workin'. Doesn't matter, 'cause the more I fit in, the easier it'll be on me. I made it through my first year at Graham without any trouble. I can make it through another.

"Just keep your mouth shut and do your work." That's what Mom said, and that's exactly what I did. Got mostly Bs, except for that C- in Algebra and D in Biology. I'm gonna take Bio again online at the library, supposed to be easier. Shouldn't have to take it again, though. I mean who the hell cares about biology anyway? *Not like I'm gonna be dissectin' frogs in the 'hood.*

All I know is, I'm gonna *stay* out of trouble. 'Cause the last thing I need is to get kicked out because I had a beef with some rich white kid. Ain't no rich kid gonna beef with me anyway. I'm an upperclassman now. Be a junior come the fall, so that makes me a junior in the summer.

I tuck my shirt back in and dive out the door. I pass by

the rail without even touching it. I'll be cuttin' it close.
Need to catch the seven-thirty bus if I'm gonna make it
to school by eight fifteen. I'm gonna have to *fly*.

Cheech and Chong

See, this bus is safe. Probably the safest bus in Florida.
Everybody on here is goin' to Milburn. So they either
live there or they work there. Or, like these two
wannabees in front of me, they're comin' back after a
night of business transactions. Yeah, to the untrained eye it
looks like they're just comin' back from a wild Fourth of
July, all messed-up lookin', hair all jacked up, bloodshot
eyes—but that ain't the half of it. Prolly got all kinds of
drugs in their backpacks.

Lots of Milburn kids go to Bandon to score. Mostly
weed, but harder stuff, too. They slum it with us po' folks
'cause they know they get the best prices in the hood.
Then they turn around and sell it to their homeys on the
other side of the tracks. And you know they get like a
hundred percent markup on the resale, for real.
I climb up the stairs of the Milburn Number One and
take my seat, up front by the window. Watchin' Cheech
and Chong make their way to the back. One of 'em
turns around and gives me a hard look, tryin' to look all
Tony Montana or somethin'. I just smile and stare at his
backpack. *Now he knows that I know.*

If I saw a couple of drug dealers on a *regular* city bus I definitely would be on red alert. But here? Ain't nothin' gonna happen. *Everybody* and their grandmama knows not to start some stuff on *this* bus. They got like a direct line to the cops on this bus. You know when you're dealing with folks who got money, they always get protected.

Don't Belong

See, *I* know that I'm half white and half black, but I know for damn sure none of these folks would *ever* think I was. When I tell people what I am, they always just look at me with that same blank stare, like I'm speakin' Greek or somethin'. Man, I'm the ultimate spy, but without all the benefits. People think I'm anything else but what I am. And they always think whatever I am, it's not as good as what *they* are. I know I'll never belong, so now I don't even try.

Familiar

This bus passes *all* the regular Bandon bus stops. We're express, cruisin' down Fullworth and over to Washington Avenue, passing Grisby Park, where I almost died last night. I shrink down in my seat, just in case. I shut my eyes like a little kid who thinks no one can see him if *he* can't see *them*.

We start to leave Bandon, but I'm never too far from

home—Mom smacks her way into my brain. Making me flinch in my seat. *Now people on this bus must think I'm crazy.* I see her hitting me over and over again. Almost feeling each blow as it makes contact.

That look on her face. Like she's possessed. Like someone else is controlling her. Sometimes she smiles when she hits me. Sometimes she laughs when I cry.

"Stop being such a baby, that didn't hurt. You're just faking. You cry like a little girl. Act like a man. You're pathetic, just like your father. Pathetic."

I can feel myself sink. Sliding down into the dark. Into that place that makes me feel so sick. That place that makes me want to go to the rail—now. It's on me so fast. Like being hit by a truck that you never saw comin'. No lights on, no horn.

I get goosebumps (not the good kind), and I feel like needles are sticking my skin—needles that I can't pull out. I hate this feeling, but it feels good at the same time. Comforting, *familiar.*

The Other Side of the Tracks
The bus slows down and sputters into a lower gear. I open my eyes and look out the window. It's like I've landed on a different planet. Concrete replaced by

green—everywhere. Perfectly manicured lawns, and
houses set way back off the street. Long winding drives
leadin' to tall iron gates.

Gated communities is what they call them. Gated to keep
people like *me* from gettin' too close to *them*. But man,
them cribs are tight. Really tight. Stucco, pucco, whatever
you call it. Every house seems like it's two blocks long
and at least three stories high. Some even bigger than
that. Even though I've been comin' here for a year, it still
makes my head spin.

I get off the bus and take a deep breath. The air clearing
my head. My eyes try to adjust to all this open space. I'm
still *so* close to Mom . . . but here in Milburn, I'm really
in another world, another universe,
living
another life.

CHAPTER EIGHT

The sprawled, lifeless body
at the foot of the stairs makes me stop dead in my tracks.
Twisted brown dreadlocks hang over this unlucky brutha's
face, making it hard to distinguish any facial features.

Lying next to the body there's an open backpack, wallet,
and a pack of cigarettes. Books and papers from the
backpack look like they were dumped out on purpose.
Kids are gathered all around. Staring, pointing, whispering
to each other . . .

A man in a gray suit is asking some of the students
questions. I walk closer to the body. My heart jumps in
my chest, accelerating from zero to one hundred in two
seconds. Kids don't even notice me. I don't notice them.
All eyes are on the body.

That dude never saw it comin'

I look down over him. *Now I can really see the bullet hole.*

"Pretty lifelike," I say half under my breath.

"We get them from Saint Katherine's. They use them in the School of Nursing. We use only the finest dummies here at the Joseph Graham Day School." The man in the gray suit smiles and puts his hand out to shake mine.

"I'm Mr. Andrews. You must be Porter, right?"

"Yeah. Jayson." *Process of elimination, right? Only brown-skin dude missin' from class.*

"You know we start at eight fifteen, right?"

"Oh, sorry, I thought summer classes started at eight thirty," I say, hoping he can't tell I'm lying, my eyes still glued to the poor brutha layin' on the bottom of the stairs.

"Okay, honest mistake. But let's not make a habit of being late," Mr. Andrews says.

I see this stuff happen for real in my hood. Out here they got to pretend. But it's still coool as hell. Forensics 1. I heard that this class is just like the TV show. *It's gonna be sweet.*

"Well, I was just getting started with my initial observations. Asking the students what they saw, their first impressions of the crime scene. What do you see, Jayson?" Mr. Andrews asks.

I see a Jamaican brutha who just got capped as he was walkin' down the stairs. Prolly came up short with this week's take, and the local drug dealer sent some serious gangstas who specialize in pain to come and collect.

That's what I wanted to say. This is how it actually came out of my mouth: "Looks like a single gunshot wound to the chest." I try to sound as official as I can. Like I'm givin' my report to the captain.

"Good, what else do you see?"

"Looks like whoever the perp was, he tried to make the crime scene look like an attempted robbery. Just from the way everything's spilled out of the backpack. It looks a little *too* on purpose." I'm in my *CSI* zone now.

"Good, Jayson. Can anyone else tell me something about the crime scene?"

Good? That shit was off the chain. Man, show some love. . . .

Back in the classroom

and my mind is wandering. I am taking notes as fast as I can, but I still can't keep up. Diagrams of bullet trajectories turn into math equations. Microscopic strands of hair left at the crime scene, footprints and blood spatter, what the dude ate for breakfast—it doesn't end.

My head starts to spin. *Can't we break for a commercial up in this piece?* Man, this class is crazy as hell. A lot more to it than I thought. I start to think about all the real bruthas I've seen with bullets in them. How I could have been one, just yesterday. It makes my stomach feel queasy. I don't want to get shot. But I *do* want to die. How and when *I* want. Nobody's gonna mess with my plan.

What plan? Do I have a plan? Never wrote it down. But I know I have one. My plan. To jump off that rail and leave this earthly body. For good. Forever. That's my plan. Not for some thug to come and bust a cap in my head when I'm not lookin'. Don't wanna end up just another chalk outline at a crime scene . . . The hell with that. I ain't never gonna go out like that.

Three-hour class

and only fifteen minutes at the crime scene. What's up with that? At least they got air-conditioning up in here. It's *way* cooler in this classroom than my apartment, for real.

Graham is like the Rolls-Royce of private schools. They don't even call it summer school in the summer. They call it summer camp. I'm sure the powers that be thought it had a more sophisticated ring to it. I wish they'd take this class outside. Not like there isn't enough space. They got like acres of land on this campus. Everything in the world is here. They got the best equipment, all high-tech stuff, brand-new computers. Three gyms, two soccer fields, tennis courts . . . They even got a lake up in this mug.

Even after a year in this place, I don't think I'll ever get used to everything they have. Man, this is a looooong way from my old school, for real. A gentle new-age hum tells me that class is over. Now *that*, I'm never gonna get used to.

My hand is sore from takin' so many notes. I shake my wrists and move my fingers to try to bring them back to life. I get up from my desk without even looking. My head makes contact with some kid's chest, pushing him back a little.

"Oh, sorry, man." My words come out automatically. You always try to defuse *anything* that might turn into *somethin'* when you live where I live.

The kid doesn't say a word. He just brushes off his chest like I had lice in my hair. He turns his back to me and walks out of class.

My first instinct

is to wipe up the floor with this kid.

My *second instinct* is to wipe up the floor with this kid.

Fortunately for him, I went with my *thirty-seventh instinct*, which was to just chill and try not to get kicked out on my first day of summer school.

Damn, he doesn't know how close he came to a *real* old-school beat down. He has no idea.

See, I know how to handle myself in this place

even though this ain't my home turf. I still have the advantage. I'm from the streets. So that means no matter how smart these kids think they are, I'm always gonna be smarter. I'm the unknown quantity. I *know* who I am, but they don't. I can turn it on and off. I can get gangsta on them in a second or talk just like they talk, if I want. I can say all the right things, do all the right things. They don't know what I'll do, if they say the *wrong* thing. For all they know I might just go "crazy" and jack them up real good, or I might just ignore them and let it go.

This kid here? I gave him a free pass. Let's see him try it again. . . . These rich kids, they think *they* have the advantage on *me*. 'Cause this is their school. Their hood. Their life. They think they're protected.

Might be, inside these walls. But they can still get got,
for real.

Lunch
The sound of my stomach growling lets me know that
I am now hungry as hell. Lucky for me I go to Graham.

I break into an almost jog as my stomach rumbles
louder. I look up to see that I've reached my destination.
The sign lookin' good enough to eat. THE HOBBER'S
CAFÉ. Yeah, that's right, they got a café up in here.

Chocolate-covered Graham
Scanning the scene in the café, I can tell already I'm
gonna be the brownest thing up in this place. Actually
I knew it before I even left the Gardens this morning. I
know this 'cause Hank Carter isn't goin' to summer
school. He's at some college basketball camp in
Indiana.

People love to live out their dreams through someone
else. That's all kids talked about at the end of school. *Did
you hear where Hank is goin' for the summer . . . ? Did you see
Hank on* Basketball Jams *last night . . . ?*

Man, all those kids love to talk about him, but I bet none

of their parents would want to live next to him, and that's
for real.

I grab a seat

next to a familiar face. "Hey, Blake, what's up?"

"Hey, Jay, didn't know you were gonna be here."

"You know, keeps me off the streets."

"Word."

Blake Evans. He tries, but he is definitely terminally
white. He's alright, though. At least he acts like I'm alive.
It's like no one here is mean or nasty to my face, they just
act like that kid in class this morning. Like they're so far
above me. Like if they touch me they might catch somethin'.

I ain't even gonna trip. I still would rather be here than
anywhere in Bandon, for real. I wasn't even jokin' to
Blake. It does keep me off the streets. And away from
Mom.

Algebra

My "catch-up" class. Man, they don't *even* play here.
You can squeeze by with a C- or D at my old school,
but here they are not havin' it. You got to get a pure C,

and that's it, no exceptions.

I ain't feelin' this class at all. And I definitely won't be feelin' it for three hours. How can they teach algebra for three hours? They call it "Intensive Math." Just another way of sayin' "Listen, dummies, this is your last chance, so we're gonna cram this shit down your throat until you get it."

Not lookin' forward to it

I look at the clock. It's sayin' that soon I'm gonna have to go back. Back to all the bullshit and gangstas and dopeheads. Back to the Gardens and Mom. Back to my life.

I'd rather stay in algebra class, for real.

The Ride Black

Watchin' the scene change from white to black, from happy to sad, from day to night.

I am lookin' out the bus window and feelin' like I always do. Like somethin' real bad could happen at any time. At Graham I know I'm safe. I can actually forget about this world, at least from eight fifteen to three thirty. Now I'm headed back to the war zone: Bandon. And the worst war of them all: World War Mom.

I am sinkin' again. Fast. Goin' down the drain. Realizing

where I'm goin', where I'm from, what I have to deal
with every day. Makes me tired. I breathe in the cool air-
conditioned air and close my eyes. . . .

I wake up quick

Gettin' hit in the head with a purse will do that.

Everyone gets pushed to the left as the bus takes a corner
a little too fast. Almost home. I check my eyes. *Thought I
was cryin'. Must have been in my dream. Dreamin' I was left
alone, in a room. Left behind in a locked room. Just me, cryin'
and screamin', not knowin' where I was. No way to get out. No
one around. No one to see if I was okay. Just me, left alone.*

The apartment is trashed

like a rock band was just here for the night and things
got out of hand. That kind of trashed. Shit is everywhere.
What the hell has she been doin'?

She's not here, but there's a pot on the stove. I turn off
the burner. The bottom of the pot is black from bein' on
the heat for God knows how long. I walk into the living
room and take a look around. It looks like a bomb went
off. Clothes and newspapers, a bunch of stuff from my
room is out here too—CDs and books. *Now, that's messed
up. Why can't she jack up her own stuff?*

I am peeling off pieces of torn-up newspaper that are

stuck to the bottom of my shoes. Inching my way closer to ground zero, feeling sicker and sicker to my stomach. *What the hell happened?* Part of me wants to stay and clean it up.

But the other part of me—the smart part—is tellin' me to get the hell out of here, 'cause I know Mom might be comin' back soon.

I change my clothes faster than Superman and get the hell out of the apartment. I slam the door shut and try not to think about what could happen, what I know *will* happen . . . when she gets back.

CHAPTER NINE

He's not home yet

Door's locked. I know his mom ain't home. No use in knockin'. Maybe I'll just wait till he gets back. He should be back soon. But what if Mom comes lookin' for me? This will be the first place she looks.

Now I'm feeling trapped. No place to go. Like a rat in a maze. *Why am I so afraid of her? I could jack her up if I wanted. I'm bigger than her. I'm stronger than her. Yeah, but she's crazy. And most of all, she don't give a fuck.*

I take my chances

and wait.

Where the hell is Trax? He should have been home from work by now. The whole seventh-floor breezeway smells like it's just been cleaned. Like with a real strong cleaner. Like what they use in hospitals or somethin'.

I lean against the seventh-floor rail, right outside of Trax's front door. Looking down, it doesn't seem that far, especially compared to eighteen. I lean over a little farther. Letting my head dangle, trying to get some fresh air. A hot air current that smells like a real bad fart hits me in the face, making me jerk my head up *fast*. A sharp pain shoots down my neck, all the way down my back to my legs.

I start knockin' on Trax's door to distract myself from the pain, and to get out some aggression, too.

"Hey, quit makin' all that racket. Ain't nobody home. Why dontcha try later?" A voice with no body shouts from three doors down.

Music and people flow out of the next-door apartment. *The party never ends.*

I keep knockin'. My knuckles start to hurt. *Maybe I can make them bleed.*

Hey, man
The sound of Trax's voice makes me jump back.

"Didn't hear you come up behind me. I've been knockin' forever. Mom lost it again. The apartment is trashed, and she's gone."

"Man, I know exactly what you need—"

"No way, Trax. We're not gonna have a repeat of Grisby Park."

"Jay, all I'm sayin' is you need to chill. Look, I'm just stoppin' by to change clothes, gonna go over to Kat's. She said she wants to try to work things out. Not gonna stay long. Really want to see Tyler, too. How 'bout you come back in a couple of hours, and we can chill. Just hang, Jay. You know, like we used to. . . . I'll hit you off on your cell if anything changes."

"Cool, man, just do what you gotta do." I try to sound like it *is* cool, but really I'm kinda pissed that Trax is puttin' me off for that ho stripper.

"Alright, see ya later." Trax rushes into his apartment and shuts the door.

Sitting on this bench

I feel like I am alone in the world. The universe. My homework and Graham might as well be a million miles away.

Mom creeps back into my head. I know she fucked up somehow, someway, and I'm gonna be the one payin' for it.

Crackyard

I am close to the Gardens but far enough away that I can see who's goin' in without *them* seein' *me*. I'm in the little courtyard just behind the parking lot. We call it the "crackyard" 'cause that's pretty much what goes down here. It's *pretty* safe during the day, but time's runnin' out now. Night is almost here, so that means the crack fiends will be here soon. They're like vampires. Waitin' for the sun to go down.

The dopeheads ain't even the ones I'm really afraid of. It's the dealers that scare me. They are *all* about the bizness, and they won't even think twice about cappin' you off, if you get in their way. And right now, sittin' on this bench? I'm in their way, 'cause I ain't buyin' nothin'. I shouldn't be here. I know it, and they know it. And soon they're gonna wonder *why* I'm here.

I already see some death dealers startin' to take up their positions. Only a matter of time before they spot me. And if they think I'm Five-0? Shit . . . That's all she wrote. . . .

Changing of the Guard

Mothers and their babies are replaced by hard-lookin' thugs slingin' rocks.

It's like everybody knows when it's time. Without sayin' a word. People just start leavin'. Like they were worker

bees gettin' the silent signal from the queen. *Time to roll,*
y'all, pass it on. . . .

Silent Sale

Hand signals and jungle sounds are the tricks of the trade.
Fingers texting on cell phones make the dealers almost
look like regular teenagers. No words are spoken. They
can't afford to be obvious about it. *Bad for bizness.* I mean,
they probably could be obvious if they wanted. Ain't like
the cops give a shit about what happens here, or what
happens to the people who live here.

These gangstas are pros. And they are *all* about the profits.
Don't even wanna take a chance with *anything* interferin'
with their paper. Sellin' their junk without sayin' a word.
It's kinda like a dance. Dopeheads stagger, barely able
to stand, defying gravity as they almost fall with every
step . . . but somehow make their way to the right spot.
Handin' off the money in a handshake. The dealer holds
up a hand sign tellin' the runner what he needs and how
much. Runner comes over, gives the dealer a hip-hop
hug, and now *he's* got the stuff. Dealer drops the stuff at
the dopehead's feet and keeps walkin'.

The dance goes on all night, every night, twenty-
four/seven/three hundred sixty-five. And no matter what
people say, it ain't never gonna stop.

I watch the show for as long as I can

but now it's really getting dark. I'm startin' to get *mad* looks from everywhere. I get up from the bench, slow, so it doesn't seem like I'm in too much of a hurry. I can feel the eyes following me as I walk away. Following me until I'm out of the crackyard and out of sight.

Like the old days

Me and Trax laughin'. At everything. Just like we used to. Just laughin' and hittin' the herb. I am watchin' Trax like he's a TV show. Just entertainment. He starts to talk some shit, and it is *so* hard to keep from laughin' in his face.

". . . Man, I told Kat this is how it's gonna be. Take it or leave it. And can you believe it, Jay? She took it. She took me back. Wants to try and start a life together. Man, this is like the best night of my life. I got my girl, my kid. See, things can get better, Jay. Things'll turn around for you, I know they will. You just have to have patience."

Poor dude, he really believes what he's sayin'. Always got to act like his life is better than mine. It's sad, really. *She's* the one who prolly said, "Take it or leave it." I know that trick doesn't *really* want him back. If I wasn't hittin' the weed so hard, I'd be tellin' Trax how full of shit he was. But I'm feelin' too good for that. I just start laughin'. Blowin' smoke in Trax's face.

He gets up fast and starts walkin' around the room, like
he's possessed. Movin' his hands wildly while he talks.
"Jay, man, maybe it was just Lonnie actin' crazy again.
Maybe he got mad at your moms and trashed the
place. You know they'll make up, and that'll be that."
Trax launches into his theory on what happened to my
apartment. I'm just stuck to his couch, not really hearin'
what Trax is saying. Not really carin'.

I just want to watch this funny-ass *Trax* show, forget
about my life, and chill. At least until the weed runs
out.

I look over at Trax

He is *out*. Passed out with a funny look on his face.
Peaceful, but with a smile. Like he's dreamin' about a joke
with a punchline that never ends. I look at the clock:
One a.m.

Reality sets in. Quick. The apartment. Mom. I'm gonna
get my assed kicked, for real.

I'm still high

as I ride up to eighteen. My buzz evaporating with every
floor I pass. Maybe it's good that I'll be high when I get
home. Might help me deal with whatever it is I got to
deal with. Might help with Mom's blows.

Maybe she's dead. That would keep me from gettin' beat.
I start to feel guilty for even thinkin' that. It's just the
weed talkin'. Yeah, just the weed.

Almost Human
As I carefully walk into the kitchen, I see something I've
never seen before: head in her hands, body draped over
the small kitchen table. Squatting over the chair, knees
bent like she wants to sit, but can't.

Jekyll and Hyde—is crying. I don't know if I should get
closer, or pretend I didn't see her and walk right out of
the apartment. There's no tellin' how she might react,
knowin' that I've seen her like this.

"I try so hard, Jay. I do. I know I'm not the best mom,
but you have to understand, Jay, it's been so hard. You just
don't know, you just don't know . . . and now . . . Oh, Jay,
honey, this is bad, this is real bad. . . ."

Honey
If she's callin' me *honey* and *cryin'* too? She *has* to be
drunk.

Now my buzz is completely gone. I flinch as she starts to
tell me her latest drama. Her latest tragedy. Her latest "I
fucked up and now we're both up a creek without a
paddle." I keep flinching as each word stings my face like

one of Mom's punches. I knew this was gonna happen. I knew it. It was only a matter of time.

Fired

1. Late too many times
2. Drunk on the job
3. Sloppy work
4. Insubordination
5. *Fill in the blank*

Mom starts to tell me her top-ten reasons for gettin' fired from her job. But I only need one:
She's Mom.

They had it in for me

"You know that secretary? Cheri? She didn't like me from Day One. I know she had somethin' to do with it. Probably spreadin' lies all around the office. And that other one, Damika, both of them are racists. Reverse racists. Had it in for me 'cause I'm white. They thought I was stuck up 'cause I wouldn't talk all that gossip with them. I was just tryin' to do my job. Told them I lived up in the Gardens, but to them the Gardens was a *good* place. Higher up than where they lived. Can you believe they thought I was stuck up 'cause I lived in *this* shithole? Can you believe that?"

I don't say anything

Just let her go. If she really wants to believe it was some

conspiracy, some crazy reverse-racist conspiracy, then she can believe that.

I know the truth. And I know somewhere deep down in her mixed-up brain, she does, too.

Mom rambles

"I've been through a lot, Jay. There's reasons why I'm the way I am. It was hard, livin' like we did. . . . So many things you don't know . . . so many things . . . I've been angry my whole life. Never can catch a break. Can't keep a job. I'm nothin', Jay. Never was nothin', never will be. . . . Shoulda just stayed in Goner, shoulda just stayed there my whole life. At least things made sense there. Nothin' makes sense anymore. Nothin' . . . I'm sorry, Jay. I'm so sorry. . . ." Mom starts cryin' again. Sayin' somethin' that kinda sounds like words, but more like garbled nonsense.

I put my arm around her and rub her back. Doin' to her what I wished she would do to me. "Don't say that, Mom. You are somethin'. And what about when you were makin' those big bucks back in the day when you used to model? You were successful, you can be like that again. It's gonna be alright, Mom. We'll be alright."

"Things aren't always what they seem—"

Mom starts to tell me somethin' but stops herself. Cuts herself off in midsentence. She shakes her head, maybe finally realizing she's being too nice to me. Or maybe she's just sobering up.

"I've had a hard life, Jay, harder than you know. Or could ever imagine. I'm tired of it, I'm just tired. . . . I'm gonna try, Jay, gonna try to change. I'll get help again, like I did before. I'll try, Jay, I'll try." Her eyes are puffy, her blond hair matted to her forehead. I feel sorry for her, I really do.

Mom wipes the tears away from her eyes, blows her nose, and goes to her room. I turn on the TV. I can hear her cryin' when I turn the volume down. I click channels and start to *sink*.

I hear the Hugheses startin' up next door. I turn the volume up, tryin' to drown out Mom and this ghetto hell I live in. I should make my escape right now. Leave before things *really* get bad. *How many times have I told myself that?*

I think about the rail, think about how good it feels when I lean against it. Think about how good it will feel to jump off of it. I want to go to it.

I almost get up off the couch, but I'm too tired. My eyes get heavy. I try to stay awake, but I can't. I dream about monsters banging on the door. Getting close.

In a sweat

on the couch, TV's still on. My heart beating fast. I forgot
to turn on the fans before I fell asleep. My T-shirt is
dripping. I go to my room and turn on the big fan by
my bed. Sticking my face as close to the blades as I can.
Warm air from the fan tries to make me cool.

I turn over on my left side, but I can't fall back to sleep.
Now I'm worrying about *everything*. Worrying about
what happens when Mom's unemployment runs out. *If
she even files for it.* Worryin' about us havin' enough
money to pay the rent, to buy groceries. . . . Hoping I
won't have to quit school and work full-time for that
cracker Bennett. Worrying about how long Mom will
stay sober this time. Knowing it won't be for long. It
never is. . . .

I toss and turn for the rest of the night. Not really
sleeping. Just waiting for the morning to come.

I am running

*I'm being chased, but I can't get away. They're catching up. The
creatures are almost to me. I don't know what they look like
'cause I ain't turnin' around. All I know is they want me dead.
They want to kill me. One of them tries to kick my feet out
from under me as I run. But I jump over it. The other
monster is throwing something at my head. I have to get away, I
have to get away. . . .*

108

I wake up in my bed

looking for the creatures in my dream. But the only creature I see is Mom. My eyes are barely open, but they're open enough to see that she is kicking me. Most of the blows are being absorbed by the pillows I just moved down to my legs.

I am trying to move, trying to get up. But she doesn't let me. Keeping me prisoner with her kicks. Now she starts punching. Punching me anywhere she can find. My arms, my stomach, my head.

Pinning me now, pinning me with her hands, her whole body weighing on my stomach. I hear myself screaming and crying.

I beg and plead for her to stop,
but she won't,
she won't
stop.
She won't
stop
she won't
stop
she won't . . .

Stop

You're my mom.

You're my mom.

Why are you doing this?

It hurts.

Why are you hurting me?

Why?

You're my mom.

You're my mom.

You're my . . .

Mom

"I told you never to write her. I told you to tell me if she
ever tries to contact you. Trina is poison. She pretended
we were all just one big happy family so she could go
and try and steal you away from me. She tried to take
you, Jay. Thought I wasn't fit to care for you. Well, I'll
show you just how fit I am. Bet them legs and that
stomach are really startin' to hurt 'bout now? Huh?
Couldn't even make it a year without that heifer tryin' to
stick her nose where it don't belong. Trina is dead to me,
so that means she's dead to you. I've told you that over
and over again, so what do you go and do? You defy me.
You deliberately defy me. Do you like this? Do you
actually like me to beat you? You must, by the way you
disrespect me all the time. You can't be this stupid. Did
you really think I wouldn't find that card she sent? Did
you really think I wouldn't find that little treasure chest
you so carefully hid in the back of your closet? You are
the lowest human being there is. I don't even think you

are human. How can you do this to me? After all I've
done for you. After what I've had to do to make sure you
had a roof over your head, food on the table. Now you
do this? You disgust me, Jay. Not only don't you tell me
she wrote you, but you tried to write her back. Tellin' her
that I was havin' more bad days than good. Tellin' her I
was drinkin' too much. How dare you? Who do you
think you are? Well, I'll tell you who you are. You are
nothin'. You'll never be nothin', either—just like your
father. You'll end up a crack fiend out on the streets,
beggin' for money. I can't handle you anymore, Jay. I
really can't. You're lucky you're goin' to that private
school today, 'cause if you weren't, I'd really be puttin'
some marks on you. Yes sir, I'd be tearin' up that hide old
school–like. You think it hurts now? Just you wait, you
ungrateful piece of shit. Just you wait."

I keep my mouth shut
It's the only way to make it stop.
It's the only way.

I feel sick to my stomach
but I have to go to school. My legs ache from being
kicked, and my stomach hurts when I touch it. I think
I'm gonna puke.

Every bump
I can feel. The bus is really haulin' now. Bouncin' over all

the torn-up streets of Bandon. Every time we hit a pot-hole I feel a little bit of puke come up from my stomach and into my throat. I want to jump out. Not even sure where I am. Don't care. *There's no way I'm gonna make it, no way.*

I finally get to school
I take the bus steps in one leap, landin' hard on the ground, which shakes up my stomach some more. I didn't need to do that.

Speed-walking on the campus path that leads to the front entrance. *Almost there, almost to the bathroom* . . . I make it to the first step—

Puke comes flying out of my mouth and all over the front steps. Yellow liquid with brown chunks comes out rapid-fire. Kids are running in every direction to get away from me. Like I had a gun and was starting to shoot.

I run inside to the bathroom. I kneel down in front of the toilet. I feel like I'm gonna die. I wish I would.

I sleep
most of the way back to Bandon. Didn't want to stick around and hear it from those rich kids. *Fuck 'em if they wanna laugh at me. They wouldn't last two seconds out here in the 'hood, for real.*

I get off the bus slow and start my walk to the Gardens. Testing out my legs and my stomach. Making sure I don't give a repeat performance. Can't afford that in my neighborhood. Throwin' up is a sign of weakness where I live. A dude could get *got* for pukin' in public. Sounds crazy, but it's true. That's what it's like livin' in Bandon— livin' in the Gardens, livin' my life:

Crazy, but true.

CHAPTER TEN

It feels like one of those made-for-TV movies
the kind where they speed up the film to show time
passing by. Showin' the sunrise in double time, moving
across the sky, representing a whole day in, like,
thirty seconds. Cars speed by on the highway, all
blurry and out of focus. Then as the sun starts its fast
nosedive, lights begin to turn on, one by one, like
popping popcorn for the eyes. Then the whole thing
starts all over again.

And again. And again

That's how my life feels now. Sped-up, movin' through
the *almost* calm, but knowin' that the storm can't be too
far off. Walkin' past the rail every day. Haven't stopped
once in the past two weeks. Mom leveling off too. Not

gettin' real drunk or high. Lookin' for work. Not beatin' on me. Best it's been in a long time, which isn't sayin' much, but maybe it's a start. Maybe.

I am trying to figure out what the hell x equals when

Bennett starts screaming in my face. Yelling about how some customer found dirt smudges on the microwave in his camper.

"You need to pay more attention to what you're doin' when you're here. If this wasn't our busy season, you'd be out on your ass, and you can take that to the bank. Now I need you to clean that Arrow over in space twenty-three. Study hall is over. Let's go, chop, chop."

I really want to tell that cracker that this is my lunch break and to back the fuck off, or I'm gonna shove some tire gloss down his throat, and he'll be shittin' wax for a year. But I just nod. This time. . . .

Not Enough Time

Goin' to summer school all week then workin' on the weekends. I got, like, no time. Not enough time to study. I *have* to get that C in Algebra. I *have* to study while I'm here. Ain't got a choice. Bennett can just kiss my black-and-white ass if he doesn't like it.

Me and Trax are sweatin' like slaves
up in this Arrow. This RV goes on forever. You could
practically get my whole apartment up in this rig. Trax
isn't sayin' much. Guess he can't put a positive spin on
catchin' Kat with some dude on her dining room table.
So much for gettin' back together.

Some things won't never change. I give him another
week, maybe two, and he'll be talkin' about gettin' back
with her.

"Look, I know you love this . . . girl, but you have *got* to
forget her and move on. If I were you, I'd take her to
court and try to get Tyler back. I mean, you guys
weren't even married. I know you ain't got no funds
for a lawyer, but at least threaten her with it. She might
get scared."

"Jay, I appreciate your concern, but you don't understand." Trax is sounding all proper. That's how he gets
when he's really mad and he hasn't been smokin' any
weed. "You don't know her. She can't help it. She got
molested as a child, and that's why—"

"Oh shit, Trax, you think that's why she blows strange
dudes on her dining room table? Is that what she told
you? You can't believe nothin' that comes out of her
mouth, man. You should know that by now."

"Just drop it, Jay, I know what I'm doin'. I gotta do what's best for Tyler, what's best for him. . . ."

"All right, I'll drop it. Just pass me the WindowShine so we can finish up and get the hell out of here."

April Figgins

winks and gives me a huge-ass smile as I climb up the bus stairs.

April is a serious 'round-the-way girl. Used to see her on the bus all the time comin' back from work. Not so much lately since I only work weekends now. She lives in the 'hood, seen her a few times at the Gardens, but I don't think she lives there. Prolly somewhere close by, though.

As the bus starts to pull away, I see April getting up from her seat four rows ahead of me. I watch her pull down her way-too-short-almost-see-through white miniskirt as she turns towards the aisle. *God, I love thongs. . . .*

I usually just keep my head down, try not to get noticed on *this* bus, but this girl has got me *all* twisted today. April is smiling, looking at me like I'm her prey, grabbing the top of each aisle seat as she gets closer. She is *fine*, though. Lookin' like a cross between Beyoncé and J.Lo. Killer body with a 3-D booty that just pops out at you and says *hi*.

The bus stops, and so does April. Right in front of my row.

"Is this seat taken?" she asks, looking right at the empty aisle seat next to me.

"It's all you," I tell her, tryin' not to sound too excited. "It's all you."

I know she sees it
I try to cover up what I know she can see. What's growin' by the second in my shorts. I stretch my T-shirt as far as it will go, pulling it almost down to my knees. Every now and then her smooth-as-silk legs touch mine as she scoots closer, then scoots away. *I know she's doin' that on purpose.*

She kinda touches her chest, too, when she talks. Like a nervous habit. I can tell she is sexual. It's like seepin' through her pores how sexual she is. I can feel it, just sittin' next to her.

I did it with a girl, once. Anna Walker. But it lasted like thirty seconds, and all she did was talk shit about me in school for the whole rest of the semester. Sayin' how I wasn't even a two-minute man . . . *What did she expect? It was my first time.* Never got back on the horse. But this chick. Daaamn, I might have to try again.

April is talkin' about God only knows what. I am not
listening to a *word* comin' out of this girl's mouth.
Not a *word*.

This is me

I get up from my seat. April pinches my butt as I slide
past her. "Hey, call me sometime." She hands me a small,
torn sheet of paper. I am *still* hard as I walk off the bus
and head home. Damn, is this ever gonna go away?

Cold Shower

Water runnin' down my back. Washing away all the sweat
from Bennett's. Thinkin' about April. *I should hit that . . .
but the repercussions, man, the repercussions . . .* Can't get away
clean with a 'round-the-way girl. She knows where you
live, where you work. She will stalk you till the end of
time. And if you get one pregnant? That's it. *Game over.*

I step out of the shower

and dry off. I hear music coming from the living room.
Laughter, too. Lonnie's over.

Stayin' out of the way

I've been stayin' out of Mom's way and she's been stayin'
out of mine. I think we get along better like that. She *has*
been readin' the want ads, lookin' for work. At least she's
tryin'.

Lonnie's over, so Mom is actin' a little better towards me than usual.

"How's that school been treatin' you?" Lonnie takes a long drag on his cigarette as he asks, so the words kind of start fading out as he inhales.

"He's doin' great. I told you my boy was smart," Mom answers for me. Soundin' like the proud parent I wish she really was.

Mom kisses Lonnie on the neck and takes a drink from her glass. *Just don't get drunk.*

I look at her and smile. I guess I'll play along tonight. If she's in a good mood, then that's good for me. Don't want to do nothin' to set her off. "I'm goin' out with Trax, see ya later."

There's no answer. I hear some moans comin' from the living room as I open the front door. Loud kissing smacks and some *Yeah, baby*s from Lonnie send me out on to the breezeway. *Man, can they at least wait until I'm out of the apartment?*

I'm not really goin' out with Trax

Just told Mom that 'cause that's who she expects me to be with on a Saturday night. Truth is, I don't know what

I'm doin' or where I'm goin'. Trax said he was goin' over
to Kat's. I think he's in full-on stalking mode, for real.
Prolly got some infrared goggles and everything.

I get out on seven

just to see if Trax is home or not. He might just be
chillin' watchin' TV.

As soon as the elevator door opens, it hits me. Except it's
real strong tonight. Man, do they got a nail salon up in
one these apartments? The smell is overpowering.
I start knockin' on triple seven—Trax's door, covering my
nose while I knock.

The hell with this, I'm outty. I turn around and head back
to the elevators, hopin' that one comes soon, so I can get
off this floor before I get sick.

I walk past the "security guard"

"Coolin' off out there," he says without even lookin'
at me.

"That's good," I answer without even lookin' at him.

As soon as I get outside I know that security guard
hasn't set foot outside the lobby 'cause it hasn't
cooled off for *nothin'* out here. Still just another hot,
muggy, smelly-ass night in Bandon, Florida.

I feel a tap on my shoulder

I know that if I was gonna get capped, I'd be dead by now. Ain't no gangstas I know be tappin' bruthas on their shoulders before they shoot them. Still, I react like anyone would. I turn around quick and put my hands up to my face.

"Yo, man, it's just me"

"You a scared boy, ain't ya? Still cute, though."

I turn around to see April Figgins laughin' her ass off at me. Barely able to speak 'cause she's laughin' so hard.

"Naw, I knew it was you. I was just playin' is all."

"Yeah, right."

April gives me that smile, like she did on the bus today. I feel myself in my pants again.

"Where'd you come from, girl? You live around here?" I try to get my cool back, but it's still far away.

"Yeah, just over on Nobly. I stay with my mom and her boyfriend." April points over her shoulder, only problem is that ain't where Nobly is.

"Cool," is all I can say, my mind goin' a million miles an hour, tryin' to figure out what the hell's goin' on here.

I don't know how it happened

but somehow me and April ended up back at my place.
She was talkin' way too much junk for me not to take
her back. Talkin' like, "Why don't we just get some beer
and chill" and "I can give you a back rub. You look
tense." And "Would it be so bad if we had sex?"

How the hell was I supposed to answer that? *Yes*, it
would be bad if we had sex? I don't think so. I'm goin'
for it. Been way too long for me. Guess it didn' take
much to wear down my defenses. *Like I had any to begin
with.*

I took a gamble that Mom would go back to Lonnie's to
finish what they started at the apartment. I was right.
Now it's time for *me* to get busy, for real.

April's got her clothes off before I can even shut the front door

She jumps up on me and straddles her legs around my
waist. I throw my keys into the air, not caring where they
land. *I'm gonna need two hands for this.*

Her tongue is like all over the inside of my mouth. On
the roof, the bottom, in between my teeth . . . *damn*. She
flicks her tongue in my right ear, making it all wet. Now
she flicks it in my left. She's practically lickin' my face off.
There is no time for small talk. Carrying her into my

room, I peel her off my waist and let her fall onto my bed. I still have all my clothes on, but I'm about to change that, right—

Now
I strip off my clothes almost as fast as April did. Throwin' my pants across the room, my belt crashes against the lamp, almost knocking it over. I throw my underwear and socks over my head, like they do in the movies.

April's body is the *bomb*. Sweet honey-brown skin, tight stomach. April gives me a wink, and I know it's about to be *on*. . . .

We both lie still
Breathin' heavy.
Not sayin' a word.
This is without a doubt the best moment of my life.
I feel like I'm in heaven,
and
I didn't even have to jump.

CHAPTER ELEVEN

Was it a dream?

My eyes fly open. For a split second I think it was all a dream. Then I feel April's naked body next to mine. I watch her sleep for a few minutes. *She even sleeps sexy . . . damn.*

I am preparing myself

for Mom busting into my room at any moment. I get out of bed quietly so I don't wake sleepin' beauty. Mom's bedroom door is wide open. She never came back last night. *Thank God.*

"Gotta go to church"

I hear April mumble as I get back into bed. It's Sunday. Sooo glad Bennett didn't need me today.

"What time is it?"

"Quarter till nine." I say, tryin' to whisper into her ear.

"*Oh shit.* I gotta go." April flies out of bed, throwing the covers onto the floor. She runs out into the living room and gathers up her clothes.

"Hey, Boo, I'll call ya later. Got your digits off your cell phone when you were sleepin'. Had a great time last night. I'll holla...." I hear the front door shut.

Boo? My digits? Oh yeah, she's a stalker. But after last night? I don't even care.

"Have a good time last night?"

Mom is standing above me. Looking down at me with a wicked smile.

"When did you get in? What time is it? I must have fell back asleep."

"I just got off the phone with Layla. She said she saw you bringin' some little trick upstairs last night. You know you're not supposed to bring people up here when I'm not home."

"Oh ... I know ... but it was kind of a last-minute

thing—"The sting of her slap makes my eyes water.
"I guess you're awake now, huh? I don't know why you
make me do this to you. Get out of that bed. *Get out of
that bed.*"

She makes me get my belt

She doesn't even let me get dressed. The sound of leather
ripping skin makes me sick. Sharp pains dance down my
back with every stroke. Tears and sweat drip into my mouth
as each blow hits its target.

She aims lower now. Down to my bare butt. The back of
my thighs. The belt digging deeper into my flesh.

Faster now, getting more for her money.
I cry out.
I cry.

Power

I look back at her face.
I don't even recognize her when she gets like this.
She looks like *she's* the one gettin' whipped.
Like *she's* in pain. . . .
I'm a man now.
I shouldn't let her beat me like this,
but
I can't stop her.
She has this power.

Power

over

me.

Mom drops the belt onto the floor

walks out of my room and slams the door behind her. My
back feels like it's on fire. I can feel the welts start to rise.

I fall onto my bed, stomach first. I bury my head into my
pillow, choking on tears and snot like a little kid. Like a
punk. My night in heaven whipped away with every
stroke of that belt.

I feel like nothin'.
Less than nothin'.
Less
than that.

It's hard to sit still

in class 'cause of my back. *She tore up my butt, too.*

"Who can tell me how we calculate the trajectory . . ."

I keep shifting in my seat like a little kid who's got
to pee. Trying to find a spot where it doesn't hurt.
There is none. I feel my phone vibrate in my pocket.
Another text from April. That makes five so far
today. . . .

Hey Boo cant stop thinkin bout u

saturday was OTC :)

hit me back when u r outta class

A

Kids still avoid me

'cause I puked on the front steps. I don't care. It's not like
they were tryin' to be my friends. Anyway, I'm here for
school, not for friends. Got a C on my last algebra quiz—
good enough for me. Class is almost through for the day.
Don't know what to do about April. She kinda scares me,
for real . . . but I *know* I won't be able to stay away. . . .
Who could?

Coast is clear

I keep my head down and walk towards the Gardens. I
didn't text April back. She's probably following me right
now. Unmarked car or somethin'. Probably implanted a
GPS chip in my balls when I was sleepin'. I start laughin'
out loud. Nobody even notices.

Apology

"I'm sorry, Jay, about yesterday morning. . . . It's just I've
been under so much stress lately. Gettin' fired and all.
Tryin' to find work. Lonnie always actin' the fool. Forgive
me?"

"Yeah, I forgive you." I don't hesitate. She'll get crazy

again if I wait too long to answer her.

It's what she wants to hear anyway. To make herself feel
better. So she doesn't feel guilty. I walk towards my room.
Mom turns to me like she was just about to give me a
hug, but at the last moment realizes she's a crazy-ass bitch
and doesn't even touch me.

I shut the door to my room, close my eyes, and try to
forget yesterday. Everything.

I try.

I take the elevator

down to Trax's, hopin' he's home. *It's after six, he should be.*
I know if anyone can take my mind off all this madness,
it's Trax.

"You must be on cloud nine"

"Yeah, I guess. Still not sure about it all—"

"What's there to be sure about, man? She's fine, she's
givin' it *all* to you, and it's *good*, right?" Trax is smilin' at
me and it's almost blinding.

"Yo, dude, when did you get a grill?"

"It's the shit, ain't it? Nelly ain't got nothin' on me."

"Man, you are so wannabe it ain't even funny." I try, but it's hard to keep from laughin'.

Trax doesn't even notice. He slides across his living room, dancin' to some song only he can hear. I slide over to him and start dancin' to some song only *I* can hear. Both of us actin' crazy. Both of us actin' like we ain't got a care in the world.

Kat walks in

like she owns the place. I can't even believe my eyes.

"We gotta go, babe," she says, completely ignoring me. "I gotta drop off Tyler at my mom's, then we gotta—"

Trax sees that my mouth has hit the floor, and tries to go into damage-control mode. "Hey, Jay, you remember Kat."

"Hey, Kat," I say as I start playing with little Tyler. He's already made his way out of his mother's grasp, and now he's standing in front of me, playin' peek-a-boo behind a chair.

"Come on, babe, we gotta go *now*." Kat doesn't even look at me as she swoops up Tyler with one hand and pulls Trax's arm with the other.

"Hey, Trax, I gotta go, too. I'll catch up with you later. Take care, man, I'll call ya tomorrow."

"I'll holla," Trax manages to yell to me as I make a mad dash out of his apartment, bypassing the elevator and heading straight for the stairs.

I look back and see Kat all up in Trax's face. About what? Who the hell knows.

I Can't Resist
316 Nobly apt 6W—8P

A

b there

J

"Who tore up your back?"
April sits up fast. Pulling the sheet down so she can get a better look.

"My mom," I answer, feeling totally embarrassed, realizing that a sixteen-year-old shouldn't be lettin' his momma beat on him like that.

"I got somethin' for that." April gets out of bed and goes to the bathroom.

"You sure your mom isn't comin' back?" I yell loud

enough for her to hear me in the bathroom.

"No, she at work, told you she won't be back till way late."

"What about her boyfriend? I feel kinda weird layin' up here in their bed."

"He's out of town all week. Just relax, baby, nobody's gonna walk in on us. It's just you and me. And Momma's gonna take good care of you."

April smiles wide as she comes back in the bedroom with a bottle of lotion. She squeezes it out onto my back; it stings at first then it feels good, cool, and soothing. "This will help it heal faster."

"Thanks" is all I can say, still feeling embarrassed.

I sit quietly while April soothes my back. Wishing she didn't have to do it, but so glad she is. So glad she's here. So glad we're together.

CHAPTER TWELVE

Hugs & kisses

and feeling close to someone for the first time. Spending
almost all week, after school, with April.

"You make me laugh," she says.

"You make me laugh, too," I answer.

"Shoot, what you tryin' to say, that I'm soft? You know I
ain't soft. You know who my set is? We the Nobly Brown
Mommas and we fixin' to kick your black'n'white ass,
you start som'in wif one us." April is talkin' her best
gangsta talk, twistin' her mouth to one side while she
speaks.

For a quick second she's pretty convincing, but then she
busts out laughing, making me bust out laughing, too. She

stops long enough to pull me close and kiss me on the lips.

"Shoot, you one fine-ass brown momma, that's all I got to say. . . ." We both crack up again, laughing so hard we can't even speak right.

April goes to the bathroom to try to stop laughing, I go to her kitchen. Neutral corners.

"Where you goin'?"
"I got to go home. Mom told me this morning she hasn't seen me much all week, and I can tell she's startin' to get mad. Wants me home for dinner tonight."

"It's Friday night, Boo, don't you want to be with me?"

"Of course. You know I do. It's just, you know, my mom. I don't want to give her a reason. I definitely don't want to do that."

Not lookin' forward to
a lot a shit. Right now I'm not lookin' forward to leavin' April's and goin' home, havin' to deal with all *that*.

Only one more week left of summer school, too; then I'm gonna have to go back to Bennett's in August, full-time until fall semester starts. Then after school starts I'm still gonna have to put in some more slave labor for that cracker. Mom still ain't got a job. She says she's got some interviews lined up but you never know with Mom. Damn, I hope she gets her shit together, and soon.

Lonnie can cook

He may be a triflin' brutha sometimes (well, more than sometimes), but that dude can cook.

I walk into the kitchen and it smells like, well, it smells like what I remember from waaay back in the day when I was small. Lonnie's got pots and pans all over the place. Music blastin' from the living room. Sounds like some old-school funk. I think it's the Ohio Players. *Yeaaaah.*

Him and Mom dance over to the refrigerator and take out some ears of corn. "Boy, you got back just in time. I think I've outdone myself today," Lonnie says, his back to me, bent over in front of the refrigerator.

"You startin' up Soul Food Fridays again?" I ask, my mouth watering from all the incredible smells.

"Well, let's just say we havin' one today. . . ." Lonnie used to have Soul Food Fridays, where he'd leave work a little early and come over and cook. That was when him and Mom were really tight, before they split up, got back together, split up, and got back together. Kinda sorta like

they are now. But maybe him cookin' today is a sign
that they're gettin' a little closer again. Not sure if that's
a good thing or a bad thing. Mom does pretty well
when she's with him, but I know she's just settin' herself
up for a crash when he acts up again and leaves her.
Or when *she* acts up and brings some random brutha
home.

Whatever. I just wanna taste some of Lonnie's greens.
They are *off the chain*.

"Why don't you go take a plate downstairs?"
Mom hands me a huge plate with everything on it.
Ham, greens, mac'n'cheese, corn bread—the works.
"God knows Carolyn don't cook for that boy." She's
talkin' about Trax's mom. "Hey, and don't be takin' that
plate to that little girl you been seein'. I don't like her. If
you ask me, ya'll been spendin' way too much time
together. You know she ain't nothin' but one of them
Bandon heifers."

"Mom, you don't even know her."

"I know the type. Believe me, I know the type."

"Get your belly swole, boy?" Lonnie breaks out his
down-South lingo on me and saves me from a run-in
with Mom at the same time.

"Yeah, it's swole—swollen and fatter than all hell." I start laughin' as I pull up my shirt and stick my belly out.

"Looks like you're about due." Mom pats my stomach, then turns and plants a huge, nasty wet kiss on Lonnie's mouth. *That's my cue, I am out.*

"Thanks, I'll take this down to Trax. Prolly stay over there a while. Cool?"

Mom takes a minute to answer on account of the fact that she's got her tongue shoved all the way down Lonnie's throat. *Man, that's all they do, eat and have sex. God, they are sooo nasty. . . .*

Lonnie looks like he's about to lose his balance, so he grabs one of the kitchen chairs to steady himself.

"Just don't be back too late. Don't want you missin' work," Mom finally says, coming up for air.

Yeah, 'cause I'm the only one makin' any money around here. You need to ask your boyfriend for a loan. You know he be sellin' weed. That's a cash bizness. Sorry-ass bustah, prolly just smokes up his profits anyway.

"Okay, I'm out."

Nobody's home
Again.

Man, Trax ain't *never* home anymore. He has *got* to leave
that girl alone.

Like a magnet
I get drawn to him. I know he could use a good plate of
food, but what am I gonna find when I get there? I never
know what shape he'll be in.

I'll holla at him real quick to see if he's home. "Hey, Pops, Mom
gave me a nice plate for ya, not sure if you're home. I'll stop
by anyway. You got my cell if you want to hit me back."

Me and Dad
"Good thing you caught me, I was just about to step
out." Dad looks like he just threw himself together. Like
he was probably stoned, or about to get stoned. Or he
was sleepin'— then got my message, so he tried to
make himself look halfway decent 'cause he knew I was
stoppin' over.

"Lonnie fix this?" Dad asks, inhaling the plate of food
like a man who hasn't eaten in days. *He probably hasn't.*
" 'Cause I *know* your moms can't cook this good." Dad
manages to get the words out in between bites of greens
and ham.

"Yeah, Lonnie's been around a lot more lately. You know Mom got fired."

"Don't suprise me. How many does that make now? She must hold the record for most times a white woman's gotten fired. I thought only black folks could get fired that much." Dad makes himself laugh, letting out a weak raspy chuckle that starts a chain reaction of coughs and almost-choking sounds.

"You okay?" I ask, wonderin' if I'm gonna have to do the Heimlich on him.

"I'm fine. . . . Too . . . many . . . cig . . . arettes." Dad coughs up the words.

Too much crack is more like it.

"Just take it slow, take it slow."

Dad leans back against his ratty-ass couch and lights a cigarette

"You sure you should be smokin' so soon after that coughin' fit?" I ask.

Dad just smiles. "Boy, you will find there are some things in life that you just can't live without. Good food, good pussy, and a good cigarette. But don't start smokin'. These things will kill ya." Dad starts laughin' again, followed by more coughin', wheezin', and a few sneezes thrown in for good measure. *Damn, he's a mess.*

"Your mom know you're here?"
I don't say anything.

"Bet she sent you over with that food, 'cause she *cares* so much about me?" Dad takes another puff off his cigarette, waiting for me to tell him what he already knows.

"No, she thinks I'm over at Trax's. She made that plate for him." I lower my head. Pops might be a crackhead, but it's still hard to get over on him.

"That's what I thought. That woman kick both our butts if she knew you brought me over a plate. She don't want me to eat. She don't want me to live. Blames me for everything bad that's ever happened to her. Bet she wishes I was dead—now don't answer that, but we both know if she had her way—"

"No, you know, she's too busy messin' up her own life to be worrin' about anybody else." I interrupt him, tryin' to make a joke.

"She still takin' them crazy pills? She need to."

"I got no clue what she's takin'. But if she is takin' some-thin', it ain't helpin'." The truth flyin' out of my mouth before I can stuff it back in.

"She still—come here boy." Before I can pull away, Dad is lifting up my shirt, tracing the Mom-made marks on my back with his hands.

"Hey, Pops, you see that game last night?" I desperately try to change the subject and pull down my shirt at the same time. But it's too late. "Did you see that catch, robbed that home run—"

Dad gets up fast, lookin' real nervous. Ignoring what I'm saying. He's got that look, like he might need a fix, and *right now*.

He starts pacing around his little apartment, lookin' like he wants to tell me somethin'. His face looks all crumpled up. Serious-lookin', with a squint—like he's tryin' to focus on somethin'. His head starts shakin' a little bit, almost like in a jerking motion. It's shakin' even harder now. He starts mumbling something under his breath. He keeps mumbling—getting louder now . . . I know what comes next.

The remote goes crashing against the window catching a little empty glass vase and knocking it to the

grimy carpet. Batteries fly out and roll, almost to my feet.
Dad is screaming. Flailing his arms.
This is what crack does.

Sometimes he loses control when he gets excited
or angry. Or emotional. It's like that part of the brain just
doesn't work right. I want to run, leave him. But he
might hurt himself, or someone else.

"See . . . see . . . see . . . she got . . . no business . . . puttin'
hands . . . see . . . see . . . I know what she say about
me. . . . I'm not, she not, we . . . see . . . It's not like all that
. . . she says it was."

Dad is stuttering, stammering, still screaming—trying to
get the words out. Almost running from one end of the
apartment to the other. I'm starting to freak out. *On the
inside.* Getting more scared, by the second.

"It's okay," I say, trying to calm him. "It's okay. . . ."

An hour goes by
An hour of Dad ranting and raving like a madman. Me
trying to calm him.
Finally he sits.
Legs still shaking.
He is out of breath.
Sweat is dripping down his face.

His stomach is bare and wet,
making his ribs look like they're sticking out even more.
Lookin' like one of those starving children you
see late at night on TV.
He starts to speak a little more clear.
a little more slow.

"Just take your time," I tell him.
"Just take your time."

CHAPTER THIRTEEN

Your Mom

"She—she, never was no model. Wanted to. Why her and Trina left Goner in the first place. But that *city*, it'll eat ya up, swallow you whole. That's what it did to Lizzie. See, see, there's—see, there's things you need to know. Deep dark things from way back that might could shed some light—I hope. I can't do much for ya, son. But at least maybe I can tell ya somethin' about your past. Maybe . . . maybe it'll help. Maybe."

I sit and listen

Dad stopping and starting like an old car that's barely got any life left in it. Barely any life left.

The words

surprise, but somehow I expect them.

Mom and Trina ended up workin' the streets, hookin' for money and a place to sleep. Sellin' their bodies at some place called Hunt's Point. *Real bad place.*

Dad was one of Mom's regulars. Then they all fell into drugs. Real bad. That's all they lived for. That's all they thought about. How to get their next fix. Dad stole while Mom and Trina sold themselves for money just so they could buy drugs.

"Didn't even care to eat. Eatin' cost too much money. . . ."

Dad is talking down into the floor while he scratches himself. First on his face, then on his arms and stomach.

"Them were the dark times. Bad times for all of us. Them were real bad times. . . ."

I'm almost numb

from this story. This tale I've heard and seen a hundred times out on these Bandon streets. But this time the story hits home.
This time
the story
hits me.

Dad stops talking and walks towards the window

looking out onto the street below. I can tell he has more to say.

"Son"

"There is one more . . . there's this one more thing that I'm not sure but . . . swore I'd never tell but . . . I feel I . . . I guess I don't have a choice."

"See"

"We was all together. You was there, too. Kinda like one big fucked-up family, livin' day to day, hand to mouth, dodgin' the law and all them guns and bullets. All of us tryin' to protect you.

"See, son, see . . . the thing is . . ."

Dad is crying

His words muffled and choked off 'cause of his tears. But I can make them out. I can understand what he's saying. His snot and guilty water drippin' from his eyes can't change what's been said. The damage is done.

Mom ain't my mom
Dad ain't my dad
So who the fuck am I?

"Stop, stop. *Stop it!* I don't want to hear no more. I don't believe this shit. You're just makin' this shit up 'cause you high. Just some dope dream you tryin' to make me believe. Why are you doin' this to me? Why?"

"Look at me"

"Jay, you think I'm gonna be an old man one day? We both know that ain't gonna happen. I'm on a road I can't get off of. I know. You know. Everybody know. . . .

"I figured with Lizzie gettin' worse and me . . . well . . . I thought time was runnin' out on us. Runnin' out on you—knowin' the truth. Figured maybe it would help—"

I run

out of the apartment. Runnin' down stairs—finally outside in the sticky, nasty night air. Crying.

How can this be true? It can't be true.

Mom and Lonnie are gone

The apartment is empty. I am alone. I walk back out onto the breezeway, wondering why he would make all that up. Letting it all soak in. Realizing . . . what if? It could be? Deep down maybe somewhere I've always known.

It's true.

Dad's words stabbing me in my brain

Trina is my real mom. Dad is not my real dad. Mom was already pregnant by the time he got to her. Nobody knows who my real dad is. Lizzie was just supposed to keep me until Trina got straight. Lizzie didn't wait. Wanted me for her own. Made me legally hers before Trina got clean. Then she took me away to Bandon, where the crackhead had kin. Lizzie stole me from my real mom. Lizzie—that monster who beats and hurts and kills me a little bit at a time—stole me away. And that crackhead who pretended to be my dad helped her. He fuckin' helped her.

Why didn't Trina try to take me back?

Why didn't she tell me *she* was my mom? All these years she had the chance to tell me, to take me back. *Why didn't she?*

I feel sick, knowing that I am just the product of a hooker and some john. The son of some nameless, faceless brutha who had enough money to buy my mom.

She never should have had me.
She *never* should have had me.

I am sliding far and fast

Sliding into that one dark place that will make it all right. Make it all make sense. Make it all go away.

I step up onto the rail, knowing that this time—this
time—*this time* . . .

April saves my life

this time.

But I let her. I let her save me. I don't know why but *this
time* I do.

April saves my life, callin' my cell, then texting
me:

I miss u :)
want 2 c u

Text in my head

I'm hangin' on by
a
thread.
I really
wanna
b
ded.
really
wanna
b
ded.

Up all night

with April. At her crib. She says she knows what I'm
goin' through, but how can she really?

I don't tell her about the rail, about how I want to die.
But she can tell that my insides ain't right.

Time seems like it's stopped but going fast at the same
time. What I found out today. How everything I ever
knew was a lie. Nothing was what it seemed. Nobody
was who they said they was. *Even me.*

"It's gonna be okay," April whispers in my ear.

I just stare up at the ceiling. Me and April together in
bed. This should make me feel better. Being with her
should help—but it doesn't.

"You're gonna be okay," April says. But she don't know
I'm just floating in space. Floating far away.

I barely get out of bed

all weekend. Staying in the same clothes. I don't go to
work. Feeling so down it hurts. Sunday night, *Lizzie's* still
gone. Maybe she's gone for good. Maybe Lonnie is really
a serial killer, and right now he's chopping her up into a
hundred little pieces and putting each piece into his
fridge, right next to the ketchup and behind the mayo. . . .

I can only hope.

Monday morning
I scrape up the last of my quarters off the top of my
dresser. Just enough for the bus.

I pull myself together. I don't want to go to class, even
though it's the last week. I don't care. Don't care about
anything *anymore*.

I feel out of control
on the inside. I feel like I'm racing a hundred miles an
hour. Everything closing in on me, like claustrophobic or
something.

Blake is waving his arms, trying to get my attention,
tryin' to get me to sit with him at lunch. I walk right
past him.

I luv u
April's text. That last time in bed, she said it to me. I
didn't say it back. Now she's texting it.

It feels good, but bad at the same time. *Good* to feel wanted,
bad because I don't even know what that word means.

Everythings gonna b ok:)
April texts me again. I smile at my phone. I text her back:

thank u

c u soon

April is tryin' to save me

even though she doesn't know it. Every time she texts, it
gives me hope. Makes me feel like maybe there's a chance
things might get better.

I sit up straighter in my seat. Even though this bus is
takin' me back to Bandon, it's takin' me back to April,
too.

She's so cool. So fine. She cares, she really does care
about *me*.

We could run away

Me and April just take off. Somewhere far away. Far away
from Bandon and those imposter parents who kidnapped
me. Away from the drugs. The past.

So far away, no one will ever find us. We could run away.
We could. Why not? What's keeping me here?

If I stay, I know that one day

one day I'm gonna jump.
And then that will be that.

But now I have April. She soothes my pain. She gives me

153

somethin' to look forward to when I get up in the morning. Something other than the rail.

I'm gonna do it. Gonna run away. As soon as I get home. Just start packin' a bag. Go swoop up April. Maybe borrow some money from Trax. He always helps me with my cell bill when I'm short. Get enough for a couple of bus tickets outta here.

I don't care where we go. It'll just be me and April. We'll get jobs wherever we end up. We can make it. With her, things can be okay. Things can change. We'll *make* them change. Be in charge of our own lives. For once, I'll be in control.

I luv u

I text her. I want to love her. *Someone.* I want to know what it feels like. Maybe if I text it, if I say it, I'll know. I'll *feel* it.

I luv u so much

I text her again.

I luv u so much 2

she texts right back.

I'll wait till I get home to tell her—no, I'll just go over to her place with my suitcase and the bus tickets. Just surprise her. Yeah, that's what I'll do. . . .

I take a deep breath as I step off the bus

inhaling the hot, humid, smelly air of Bandon. Hopefully for the last time. Gas fumes from the bus pulling away make me cough, but I don't mind. Not this time. I've got a big shit-eating grin on my face, knowing that I'm about to change my life. Leave this place and never look back.

I text April as I walk.

b over soon.

Something ain't right

Sirens are blasting more than usual. People are running towards me. Everybody's on their cells. I get a real bad feeling in the pit of my stomach.

I am calm at first. "What happened? What's goin' on?"

Then I start to panic, yelling at people to answer me. "What the hell's goin' on? What the fuck happened?"

Nobody answers. I start running.

Ambulances and fire trucks

Cops are everywhere. This is *not* good. I am sprinting now, as fast as I can towards the Gardens.

There's over two hundred apartments in this place, but somewhere, way down inside of me, I know where it is. I know who it is. I know it's Liz—I know it's Mom.

CHAPTER FOURTEEN

Thick black smoke
is billowing from the west side of the Gardens. *My side of the gardens.*

"You live here?" A big burly white cop puts his arm up and stops my forward progress.

"Yeah, what happened?"

"Explosion. You can't go any farther. We're evacuating."

"What explosion? Where? What apartment? Tell me what apartment. . . ."

Can't be real
The words the cop is saying, the name I'm hearing from tenants and friends.

Not believing. Not wanting to believe what is happening.
This can't be real.

Layla

is runnin' towards me, tears streaming down her face. She
starts hugging me, screaming something. She's hysterical.
Can't make out a word she's saying.

I pull away from her, pushin' her away. I have to get in. I
have to.

"Damage was limited"

"Fortunately the damage was limited to one apartment. It
is still unclear as to what caused . . ." I run past the cop
and stand staring at the news reporter. His perfectly fake
hair doesn't move. Talking calmly like this is nothin',
like this just happens every day.

I don't hear the rest of what he says. *He doesn't care. Just
another tragedy in the hood.* . . . I want to kill that news
reporter, I want to kill that cop.

I've got to get in. I run as fast as I can towards the lobby.
In seconds, I feel strong hands pulling me from behind.
Trying to pull me down.

Now they are pushing me forward. I am falling over. My
face is smashed into the ground. My arms feel like they're

being pulled out of my shoulders, cuffed so tight behind my back, it makes me scream.

Must be four or five cops on top of me. I wish they would just shoot me, just get it over with. Put me out of my misery, once and for all.

CHAPTER FIFTEEN

There's this place

This place that you go to when reality becomes too
much. When what you see is more than you can take.
That out-of-body, floating-over-everybody experience,
but at the same time it's still me, feet on the ground.
Standing in this spot. Like being the first and third person
in a book. Like what Ms. Corcorian was teachin' us last
year. "Point of view."

Right now I am first and third person. I know I am me,
Jayson Porter. But I am also floating above this reality that
can't be real. Seein' everything . . . seein' me . . . standin' . . .
watchin' this horror show all around me. This white room
with masks and machines. Strange noises and the smell of
clean death. I feel myself losing my balance, dizzy, like I
just hit the chronic *real hard*. I sputter from high above.
Still floating, but looking for somewhere to land.

"He can hear you"

the woman whispers in my ear, looking almost like someone I know, but not quite.

The sound of artificial air being pumped into Trax's lungs
makes me queasy. I don't want to get too close to his
bed. I don't want to get too close.

He's not gonna make it

I know he won't. Burned over most of his body. He's in a
coma. Can't breathe on his own.

I see how the doctors and nurses are looking at him. At
us. *Only a matter of time . . .*

The woman who whispered in my ear all of a sudden
becomes familiar to me. *Trax's mom.* She's crying,
touching his forehead. Wanting to stroke his face, but the
tubes are in the way, so she strokes the air above his face.

Tubes and machines are attached to every part of his
body. I can't even tell it's him in there. I have to tell
myself that somewhere, underneath all of that stuff, is
my friend.

April squeezes my hand

as we walk out of his room. The woman playing the part
of my mom looks like she hasn't slept in days. Layla has

her arm around her, all of us moving like we're stuck in quicksand.

I look back into Trax's room one last time. Doctors and nurses are leaning over his bed, moving frantically. His mother is screaming.

April kisses my cheek. I don't feel anything. No sadness, no anger—nothin'. I am numb.

Mom/this woman/the kidnapper is talking a mile a minute in the car

"That's why I've always told you, Jay, got to stay away from drugs. That's how you'll end up. Meth is the worst, too. Them chemicals they use, so unstable. Just an accident waitin' to happen. Should've known, with how it always smelled down on seven. Like fingernail polish remover. You know that's one of the smells them chemicals give off. . . ."

"I feel so bad for Carolyn, she had no idea. None of us did. I mean, we all knew there were druggies livin' up in that apartment next to Trax, but who knew they had a whole meth lab goin' on in there? It's just a shame. Just a shame. Poor little Tyler. It's always the children that get left behind. Always the children . . ." Layla starts crying, her words choked off as she wipes away her tears with one hand, the other on the steering wheel.

Sitting in the backseat of Layla's car, all I can think about is what went through Trax's mind when it happened. What was the last thing he thought about?

Sleep comes and goes

but the reality is always there. Ready to smack me upside my head when I wake up. Trax blew himself up doin' meth. Trax *and* his girl, Kat, blew themselves up. Prolly was doin' it next door for months. *She* prolly got him into it. Guess I'll never know. *Well, she got hers in the end.* Poor Tyler, got no mom or dad. Sounds familiar. . . .

I just keep goin' over what happened. Like they're just facts in some textbook:
Trax was doin' meth.
Trax was doin' meth in a meth lab in the apartment next door to his.
Trax blew himself up doin' meth.
He hid it from me.
I should have known.
I should have stopped him.

I won't ever see him again.

Hours bleed into days

Getting up only to go to the funeral. Everything like a bad dream. I see bits and pieces, but it's fuzzy, blurry, out

of focus. The kidnapper, Layla, Lonnie, and April. I know
I see them—but they don't seem real. Nothing does.

**They say I can make up the classes/the kid-
napper still doesn't have a job/ Bennett says
I can come back when I'm ready/ things go
back to . . .**
Nothing will ever be normal. I slip deeper and deeper,
sliding as far down as I ever have. I pass the rail,
wishing I had the strength.

CHAPTER SIXTEEN

Three weeks

and I feel like I've finally woken up. The nightmare is
over. I am happy, knowing that today is the day. The best
day of my life. The day I am going to die.

I grab the card Trina sent to me, all taped up from where
Lizzie ripped it, and stick it in my back pocket. *Now we
will always be together—mother and son.*

April calls me, her voice sounds so cheery and upbeat.
She loves me so much. I love her, too, but April can't save
me. Nobody can. This is the only way, I know that now.
I'm strong enough to see what has to be done. I feel so
good today. Like a weight has been lifted off me. I am
happy. Finally, I'm happy.

I meet April for coffee

She looks extra hot to me. Her beautiful body almost bursting out of her clothes. We drink our coffee and walk back to her place. I rip her clothes off and she rips off mine. We make love all day long.

It's quarter till five

People will be coming home from work soon. I want them to see. I want everybody to see.

I've done it so many times in my head before. I know what will happen. I know this is the best way.

I stop over to see if Trax is home before I go up to eighteen.

Man, he ain't never home.

Crawling under what's left of the yellow police tape, I wait for a while.

Prolly over at his girl's place. Tryin' to get back together. Why won't he leave her alone?

Leaning out over the seventh-floor rail. I wait and think about what it will feel like to be free. To finally be free.

I can't wait to go home. I know Trina's gonna have some good food waitin' for me right when I walk in the door.

I look down.

*I'm gonna do it here, right in front of his apartment.
I prolly won't even make the papers. Just another statistic from
another broken home, another broken life. . . .*

*Wish I could see the look on the kidnapper's face when she finds
me on the ground . . . wish I could take her with me. . . . The
crackhead's really gonna need a fix after they scoop me up off the
pavement. . . .*

I look over at Trax's front door, Lucky 777, *hopin' it will open.
Hoping he will come out and ask me if I want to watch the
game or if I want to hit some weed.*

I start laughing. Laughing and crying at the same time.

*Man, you know how you get when you hit the weed. Slow
down, Trax. I ain't tryin' to get in no beef again on account of
you. Man, you are a trip, for real.*

"Trax." I say his name out loud. It sounds so different
now.

I'll miss you, Boo, I'll really miss you. . . .

"WHAT?" I thought I heard April's voice. "April," I whisper into the air.

I love you, April, I really do love you. . . .

I climb up onto the top rung of the rail. I start to lose my balance but I catch myself at the last second. I spread my arms out as far as they'll go. I shut my eyes, knowing that in seconds the pain will be gone forever and I'll be free.

Finally, I'll be free. . . .

after

CHAPTER SEVENTEEN

I am a bullet

screaming to the ground.

The air rushing past me, so fast I can't breathe.

I am gasping.

The sound—like a 747 taking off in my eardrums.

Getting louder and louder.

The ground getting closer and closer.

This is supposed to get rid of my pain,

get rid of it forever.

This is my cure.

It

HURTS.

It wasn't supposed to hurt.

I was supposed to go unconscious.

I haven't passed out yet, and it hurts.

It hurts 'cause I can't breathe.

My chest collapsing against itself,

squeezing all my insides
OUT.

Squeezing *everything*.

The building an upside-down blur, balconies racing
past me.

Going even faster,
my eyes blasted open from the force of gravity.

I try to blink, but I can't.

My speed
much faster than I planned.

I flip over . . .

Feet first,
I start my reentry into the next life.

I really hope it's better than this one.

I can see a woman pushing a stroller—
a man jogging—
people
living—

life.

I am watching the ground
getting bigger and bigger. . . .

I don't
wanna
die.

It's too late.

Why did I do this?

I don't want to die.
I want to see
April again.
I want to feel her skin.
I don't want to die.
I scream the words, but I can't hear a sound.
I don't want to die.

CHAPTER EIGHTEEN

B

l

a

c

k

CHAPTER NINETEEN

S

i

l

e

n

c

e

CHAPTER TWENTY

I am dead
I have to be.
I can't see or hear.
I am in
Nothing-
ness.
I am

dead.

CHAPTER TWENTY-ONE

The pain
is fucking horrible.
The pain is telling me that
I'm *not* dead.
That somehow, someway,
I survived jumping from seven stories up.
I try to move
but
I can't.
Faces are in my face.
Lips are moving,
people are all around me.
Then everything goes . . .

CHAPTER TWENTY-TWO

. . . black again
I can't hear.
I can't
br
ea
th
e.

Now
I must really be

CHAPTER TWENTY-THREE

Dead

CHAPTER TWENTY-FOUR

Heaven or Hell

I just hope my elevator goes up . . .

I just hope my elevator goes up . . .

I just hope my elevator goes up . . .

I just hope my elevator goes up . . .

I just hope

my

elevator

goes . . .

He's back

"We've got a pulse. Heartbeat is . . ."

. . .up
I just hope my elevator goes up.
I just hope my elevator goes—

"Just relax, you're going to be okay. Try not to move.
Give him three-hundred cc's of . . ."

I just hope . . .

Blurry ghosts

come close then fade away, trying to suck my blood. Aliens
probing my body, moving me to their spaceship. I don't want to
leave.

Please don't hurt me. Please.

CHAPTER TWENTY-FIVE

I wake up to bright lights
and beeps
and
strange faces.
I can smell my
own shit,
and
pain
is
everywhere.
I can't escape it.
I try to sit up and struggle.
Try to fight my way out of here,
but I can't lift my head.
I can't lift my body.

The same song playin' over and over again

The canopy . . . the hood of the car . . . the way he landed . . .

HE WAS SO LUCKY

HE WAS SO LUCKY

HE WAS SO LUCKY

HE WAS SO LUCKY

HE WAS SO LUCKY

HE WAS SO LUCKY

HE WAS SO LUCKY

HE WAS SO LUCKY

HE WAS SO LUCKY

HE WAS SO LUCKY

HE WAS SO LUCKY

HE WAS SO LUCKY

HE WAS SO LUCKY

HE WAS SO LUCKY

CHAPTER TWENTY-SIX

Still touch and go

"The injury's caused his brain to swell. We'll have to watch him close."

closecloseclosecloseclose

CHAPTER TWENTY-SEVEN

Strong winds

blowing and the leaves look like they're clapping. Clapping for me. . . . The wind is blowing in my face, blowing down my throat, making me choke. . . . Walking uphill trying to get somewhere, but I don't know where. Nothing looks familar . . . strange sounds and voices are coming from just over this hill, this hill that ain't got no beginning or end. . . . (I smell bacon cookin'.) I've been trying to walk up this hill for hours, I don't know why I can't get any further. The voices are getting louder, but I still seem so far away. . . .

I'm home, Mom

Trina gives me a kiss and a big hug. Made a ham with all the fixin's.

Are ya hungry?

I'm starved, Mom. I'm starved.

I sit down at the long dinner table. The smell of sweet flowers mixes with the smell of cornbread and greens. I look at all the incredible dishes laid out for me to eat. Fresh snap beans, sweet potatoes, scalloped potatoes. Mouth is watering . . . so hungry . . . so hungry . . .

How was your day, Jay? Jay? Jay? Jayson . . . ?

Jayson

"Jayson, can you hear me? Can you hear me?"

My eyes fly wide open, then close again.

"Stay with me now, Jayson. Stay with me. You're in the hospital. We're going to take good care of you."

Feels like I've been underwater for a real long time. I try to pull off the mask that's on my face, but I can't reach it. I cough into the mask. *Can't get enough air, must still be underwater.*

"Jayson, just try to breathe normally, just try to relax." Loud voices shouting into my head. Lights shining into my eyes. Something warm going into my arm. It burns a little.

I feel my body start to s l o w down. Breathin' gets easier.

Mom, is that you? It time to eat yet?

CHAPTER TWENTY-EIGHT

Time

I can't tell
time.
I can't tell how long,
how many
hours
days
weeks
months
minutes
seconds.
I can't tell
time.

CHAPTER TWENTY-NINE

I feel something around my neck

It's a snake. I can't breathe . . . I can't move my head. It's trying to kill me.

"It's to keep your neck from moving," the voice says.

I touch the snake. It itches. Feels like plastic. No snake.

She's a nurse . . . in the hospital.
I'm alive.

My feet feel tingly. *But I can feel them. I'm alive.*

"We're going to put you in traction now, Jayson"

"This will help to stretch your spinal cord. Your neck has been fractured. And we need to relieve some of the pressure and swelling before we can operate. Do you understand?"

There's a brown-skin Santa with a long white beard up in my face, and he's talkin' real fast. I'm just about to tell him that he's a little early for Christmas when . . .

A whole team of people come and lift me off my bed

and onto another. *My head's in a sling. I hear clanging— movement around my feet. Jolts of electricity—shooting down my right arm. My shoulders—my hands HURT. AAAAA- HAAAHAAAOW! It hurts sooo bad.* . . . The nurse gives me a shot into the skinny tubes sticking into my hand.

"This should make a world of difference," she says.
I feel better. I feel bett . . .

I wake up in a different room

"You were in the ER, now you're upstairs . . . It's called cervical traction," the brown–skin Santa says. *Pullies, weights stretch my spinal cord . . . surgery . . .* Santa is talkin'. I think I'm listening. I can't tell. *Three days I have to be in traction, or is it two? Small weights—thirty-five pounds?* I hear what he's saying, kind of. I'm in and out of sleep and awake. . . . *Monsters and aliens keeping me from moving my neck . . . my head . . . Why won't they leave me alone?* The pain comes, then goes.

"Nerve pain," a voice says. "Don't wait until the pain gets so bad. Push that button, that's what it's there for." The nurse is looking down at me. Her mouth is closed, but somehow I can hear her words. *Another alien . . .*

I push my pain button, but I waited too long. *Eyes heavy, blurry. So tired, so tired . . .*

CHAPTER THIRTY

My eyes are open

or at least I think they are. Feels like my brain is catching
up, coming back to me . . . Back in my head, not somewhere else . . . lost in space . . . Putting it all back together
again, words and meaning—where I am . . . but *something
is still different. Something still doesn't feel right. . . .*

It's like I just went to sleep

but I think it's the next day. The nurse tells me it's really
the day after that. She says I've been sleeping a lot, on and
off, because of my injuries and the pain. "It's okay," she
says. "It's normal."

The first face

I see is Dad. He's high—breath stinks. But it's so good to
see . . . But then *I remember. I remember,* the truth coming
back. Back from the dead, just like me. *He's not my dad.*

He's not my dad.

"How you feel?"
he asks.

I am looking straight up, 'cause that's the only way I can
look. Stuck with this thing on my neck. Held hostage by
Dad's—this man's—horrible breath. If I wasn't so jacked
up I'd prolly gag. I press my pain button, three times—
quick. "I . . . I . . . I . . . I . . . I'm . . . Aaaaaah-aaaaaaah. . . ."
My mouth feels dry. Feels like my lips are stuck together,
*no that ain't it, its somethin' else. I can't get the words out . . .
I'm alive, I'm alive, I'm just glad to be alive. Why can't I say
it?* It's like I've got it all together in my head, but when I
try to talk . . . somethin' fucked up happens.

"That's okay, son, don't try to talk. Docs say you gonna
be just fine. They say you were lucky. Real lucky."

Where have I heard that before? The man who used to be
my dad leans in close to my ear, whispering, with a
crazy-serious look on his face.

"I'm so sorry, Jay, you know, about the other day . . .
about *everything.* I knew it wasn't right—stealin' you away
like that when you was a baby. But your momma—
Lizzie—she was so set on it. Said we could give you a
better life than Trina could. Said that Trina would never

199

come back for you. I knew that was a lie. I knew Trina was gettin' straight. Knew she would come back for you . . . I knew Lizzie was wrong. I knew the whole thing was wrong but Lizzie was so strong . . . I was so weak. . . . I know all this ain't gonna help much now but If I'd known all those years ago that you'd end up—"

He starts crying, coughing up his words. "Your momma's—Lizzie's—outside, so I'm gonna get outta here. I'll be back, son, you know I'll be back. . . ." He looks weak and feeble, like a man twice his age. Lookin' like he might just keel over right here and now. I watch him half stagger out of my room, listening to the rhythms of his sniffing and coughing as he walks out. I push the pain button. . . . Sleep is on me before I know it. Sleep is on . . .

Lizzie
I feel her tears dripping down onto me. Rolling down to my lips. I keep them closed tight, like my eyes. *Maybe if I don't open them she'll go away.* The smell of liquor and stale cigarettes gets inside my nose and stays there.

"You're gonna be fine, baby, you're gonna be fine."
She stands over me, looking at me. Holding my hand, touching my face—

"Kkkkid . . . nnnnnap—kkkkid . . . nnnnapppper."

200

The word feels like glass cuttin' its way up my throat and out of my mouth.

For a split second Lizzie's expression changes. She looks confused. Almost scared. I feel her grip on my hand tighten. It's like her whole body freezes. But it only lasts a few seconds and she's back. Back to the role she's been playing my entire life. *And the winner for best actress in the role of Jayson Porter's mom goes to . . .*

I feel pain knifing its way down the left side of my body. My face tightens. I start to sweat. I push my pain button. I push it again.

She's gone
It's like I just nodded off for a minute, and when I woke up she was gone. Lizzie, the kidnapper—

I'm glad.

CHAPTER THIRTY-ONE

AAAAAAAAaPPppppppppppppril
The name comes out all jacked up, so I say it again.
"AAAAAAAAaPpril. Mmmmmm mmmmmy Ggggg
Gggggggirl . . ."

The nurse gives me a strange look at first, then nods her
head like she understands. "Let me go check and see if
she's here."

"Th-th-th-th-anks."

I expect April to come walking into my room
but she doesn't. It's just the nurse. "Sorry," she says. "Dr.
Iram will be right in to see you." The nurse does something with one of my tubes and walks out of my room.
Where is April?

Doctor Iram, aka the brown-skin Santa, is telling me

he will be the one operating on me. "I'm a neurosur-
geon, and I'm the one who's responsible for putting
you in this thing. Lots of fun, huh?" Dr. Iram is smiling,
but I'm not. "We've had to keep you in traction a
little longer than we'd anticipated, but I think I'd like
you to be in traction one more day, then we'll operate."
Dr. Iram is talking and examining me at the same
time. "When you wake up you'll be in what we call
a halo."

Oh shit. That's that Frankenstein thing.

"You'll probably have to wear it for three months or so,
but it could be a lot worse, Jayson."

*Startin' to feel tired again, the pain—comin' back. Have to stay
awake . . . Have to hear what he's tellin' me. They brought me
back, saved my life more than once. . . . Fractured neck at the
C5-C6. Head injury—hopefully no permanent damage—
cracked ribs, fractured bones in my right arm and wrist, broken
right leg . . . multiple contusions . . .*

"Jayson, you really need to know, not only are you lucky
to be alive, but you're lucky that you aren't completely
paralyzed. We have to go in and fuse those bones in your
neck to make sure that you *don't* become paralyzed, and

so that you can live a normal life again. . . ."
Paralyzed, lucky to be alive.

". . . You'll start physical therapy right after surgery to
help you get stronger and to help you get used to wear-
ing the halo. As for your speech, you'll be starting speech
therapy, as well, which should help a great deal. It should
get better, but there are no guarantees, Jayson. It appears
you suffered a mild traumatic brain injury. We think that
is what's causing the stuttering, however we haven't ruled
out emotional trauma, either. I know it's frustrating since
all of your other cognitive functions appear to be working normally. You may experience other symptoms in the
coming weeks and months, so you need to tell someone
if you feel there is any change in your mood or thinking.
Otherwise, you'll just have to work hard and be patient.
It's all going to take time, but you will get better,
Jayson."

Doctor Iram has a way about him when he speaks.
Somethin' that you notice right off. *He really believes what
he says. I like that.*

This is Doctor Zargis

"He'll be the doctor you talk to." Dr. Iram pats Dr. Zargis
on the shoulder and smiles. "You guys can talk about
whatever you want. Anything—music, girls—"

Dr. Zargis smiles. "Well, my advice about girls might be a little dated, but I'll do my best."

"Don't let him fool you. This guy is the hippest dude on staff. I'm sure you guys will get along famously. We'll leave you now so you can get some rest."

Doctor Zargis looks right at me. Like he knows me. Like he knows what I've been through. Without saying a word. He looks like he understands. I watch the two doctors leave my room. Lookin' like two white sheets blowing on a clothesline. *My pain meds must be kickin' in.*

A woman in a business suit wakes me up
She's talkin' to me, but it's like I just came in, in the middle. I'm lost.

". . . I know they were here a couple of days ago, but since then we've been unable to contact either of them. Do you know how we could get a hold of them? We do have consent for your surgery, but there are other matters we need to speak to them about. Do you know of another phone number where we could contact your mom?"

I stare up at her, looking at her like she's from another planet. The nurse comes in to do what she does. She whispers something to the woman in the business suit.

"Okay, I'll come back later, but we really need to resolve this," the business-suit woman says, and walks fast out of my room.

CHAPTER THIRTY-TWO

There is something on my head
It feels heavy
and it's

freaking me out.

It's big
and it's

freaking me out.

Even though I know
what it is,
it's still

FREAKING ME OUT!

The day after surgery. I am officially Frankenstein

Pins in my new fifteen-pound head. Bars attached to a
plastic vest with fur under it. Can't move my head up or
down. I am locked into one position (all the time)—
straight ahead. I panic. I feel like I have no control over my
head. *Claustrophobic.* Like I'm locked in this thing, no way
to escape for three months. My heart is speeding up. My
hands are shaking . . . sweaty, too. . . .

"Just take deep breaths, you're doing just fine. I know it's
kinda scary at first, but you'll get used to it. Just try to
relax," the nurse says as she struggles to keep me and my
big-ass Frankenstein head from falling over. "That's it,
Jayson, move everything all at one time. Think of yourself
as one piece that has to move at the same time. Good,
everything at the same time. That was good, Jayson, real
good. Let's get you back into bed, get you dried off.
You're soaking with sweat."

I want to see April

but I don't know where she is. I heard she came to see
me once when I first got here. But that was when I was
out—*unconscious* . . . I can't believe she won't come see
me. *Why won't she come see me?*

CHAPTER THIRTY-THREE

It hurts
to stand up
to sit down
to piss
to shit
to eat
to drink
to get clean
to move too fast
or
too slow.
It just
fuckin'
hurts. . . .

CHAPTER THIRTY-FOUR

I cry a lot now

I cry because I'm in pain. Not just physical. But on the inside, pain. It helps to take my medicine for this depression that I have, but none of it changes what happened. None of it brings Trax back, or takes away all the years of Lizzie's beat downs . . . and the big lie that was—*is* my life. None of it brings April into my room to hold my hand. I miss her kiss and her touch. I MISS HER . . .

I am waiting

for someone, anyone, to visit me. The crackhead, Lizzie— I don't care, just someone. I can see the look on the nurses' faces. They feel sorry for me, sorry for the boy who tried to kill himself. And now he's been abandoned. *Again.* The business-suit lady is hovering around my room. I can't see her, but I know she's there. I wonder if they're gonna kick me out. *Who's gonna pay my bills? How am I gonna get out of this halo if they kick me out?*

CHAPTER THIRTY-FIVE

You jumped, Jayson, *you jumped*

Dr. Zargis always corrects me. He says I can't shy away
from the truth. *The truth will heal.* I try to talk, but it still
comes out wrong. Jumbled and stuttered. I hate how I
sound.

"I did-did-did-didn meee me . . . mean—sli-slip-slip . . ."

"*Did* you slip Jayson? You told me before that you
meant to jump. You said you wanted to stop the pain,
remember? You said it was only after you jumped that
you realized you wanted to live."

"M-m-m-may-may-may-be . . . D-d-d-d-don-don't
member. . . ."

"Maybe you don't want to?"

CHAPTER THIRTY-SIX

I want to kill Gary, my PT dude

He is straight from Abu Ghraib prison, for real. *Bastard.* I think he makes me do more than the other patients. Seems like I do more walking. At least I got those two bars to hold on to. *Does this dude know I still got a broken leg on top of everything else? How many times can you go up and down three steps?* Can't get away from him, either. He's attached to me by a belt. After I'm done doin' what he says, I feel like I did two weeks ago, when I first got in this place. He says my back is getting stronger, my legs are getting stronger. He's always talkin' about me gettin' stronger. *I hope he drops dead right now.*

Speech

therapy. Learning to speak again, almost from scratch. Man, I feel like a punk. But Cindy is cool. She says I'm gettin' better, too. I don't know, I think I still sound stupid.

I am so tired

by the end of the day. By the end of the week . . . from PT and speech therapy and just tryin' to function like I am . . . But I know I am lucky to be alive. And I know I should be thankful that I am alive, but it still hurts and it's still hard. Everything is so hard.

CHAPTER THIRTY-SEVEN

I hate this halo

I wish I could just rip it off. But you can't. I've tried.

It's so hard to sleep

wearin' this thing. I can only lie on my back. The nurses say I can sleep on my side—yeah right, I'd like to see them try. I got all kinds of pillows behind me. I don' think I'll ever get used to it. Sometimes I get dizzy if I get up too fast. Wakes me up in the middle of the night. The pins are just uncomfortable as hell. My arm hurts worse. Sometimes if I move I get a *ZING*. Instant pain. A little to the left—*ZING*. A little to the right—*ZING*. Found out the hard way about nerve pain. It fuckin' hurts. And my nerves are still *all jacked up, so I hurt a lot*. . . . Supposed to get better over time just like everything else. . . .

CHAPTER THIRTY-EIGHT

It must have been terrible

to find all of this out. It shook you to your core, it just
must have been awful. You find out after all of these years
that your father isn't your biological father, your mother
isn't your birth mother. You've had to deal with so
much, so much, Jayson . . . from your mom, seeing your
dad the way he is . . . always wondering if he was alive or
dead. Losing your best friend . . . Our brains are just not
equipped to be able to deal with so many horrible things
stacked on top of each other. Let yourself feel the pain,
it's okay. Give yourself permission to say, *It's okay, I'm
okay, I'm not a bad person for jumping*. You can't take it
back, but we can learn from it. We can learn why you did
what you did. You've got a second chance, you've got
your whole life ahead of you. You're going to get better,
inside and out. You already are getting better. But you
need to admit it, not just to me but to yourself. You have

to admit, own it—what you did. Set it free, Jayson, set it free. . . .

I am sitting in my chair

My head propped up against the wall. *Dr. Zargis would have made a great lawyer.*

I feel the tears roll down my cheeks, moving so slow. I want to wipe them away, but I'm too tired. I'm just too tired.

Dr Zargis is staring at me

Silent, waiting for me to say it. Waiting for me to say . . .

I- I-I-I jjjjjjjj-

ummmmm-ped.

Tears

and Dr. Zargis gives me a careful hug. "This is a great first step. This is very important. I'm proud of you, Jayson. I'm very proud."

CHAPTER THIRTY-NINE

This is Mrs. Phelps
She's from Social Services.

This is Mrs. Williams
She's from Our House.

This is
Officer Lawton.

I want to turn it off
Turn it all off. The voices and what's gonna happen next.
I shut my eyes and try to turn it off. I don't want to see
these people, hear them tellin' me what my life's gonna
be, where I'll have to live, what I gotta do. I don't wanna
hear it. I don't wanna know.

Police report

Lizzie and Lonnie are gone. My fake dad, the crackhead, is missing, too. There are no leads.

My report

I'm still here, but April isn't.

CHAPTER FORTY

Everybody says I'm getting better
Doctors and nurses and PAs and techs and orderlies and
janitors and even random dudes who wander into my
room by mistake. It's like people just say it automatically.
You're gettin' better, you're gettin' better.

All I know is I still stutter, I'm still lookin' like
Frankenstein, and I don't know where the hell I'm gonna
go once I get outta here. *I ain't goin' to no damn foster
home, that's for damn sure.*

I think maybe all of them are just sayin' I'm gettin' better
so they can kick me out. Prolly used up the last of the
emergency insurance money for abandoned kids like me.
Prolly want me outta here and *quick.*

CHAPTER FORTY-ONE

Dr. Zargis looks impatient
I know I'm leaving soon, and he knows it, too. He's worried about me. I'm worried about me.

"What is it, Jayson? Specifically?"

"Ev-ev-ev-rything . . ." I answer.

"What is everything?" he asks, his voice sounding calm. But I know he's getting frustrated. *I'm getting frustrated.*

"Nnno, Mmmomm, Ddddadadad, Trrrraaaax, wh-wh-wh-wh-ere aaa amI gggoggo nnna ggggo? Wh-wh-wh-wha-t's gggoggo nnna hhhhahhhhpppppen tttt to-me? I-I-I-I-I'm ssssss sc-sc-sc-sca sca-sca-scared."

"It's okay, Jayson, you're going to be fine."

"You're feeling powerless again, because things are just happening to you and you have no control. That is a very scary situation. Your feelings are founded, Jayson. It's okay to be scared.

"But don't let those feelings overpower you. These are some of the same feelings you had before, when you decided that there was only one choice left for you. Remember?

"But things are different now. You have a support system now. You have me. My door will always be open to you, Jayson. It may not seem like it now, but you *are* going to be okay. Being away from your home and your mother may the best thing for you at this time.

"Think about the positives, Jayson. You've come such a long way in just a few weeks. We'll be setting you up with another therapist as part of your outpatient treatment. In addition to your therapy, I also want you to have a way to get out your emotions. A clear and concise way, one that doesn't require you to struggle so much with your speech. I think writing down how you feel could be very beneficial to you. What if you kept a journal? Would you like to do that?"

I nod, which is not an easy thing to do when

you're wearin' what I'm wearin'.

"I have a little present for you. Now that your wrist is healing, I think you'll be able to handle this just fine."

Dr. Zargis gives me a tan bound journal with a cool design on the front cover. It's a circle with different colors and shapes inside of it. Then another smaller circle with the letter J inside of that. *Cool.* It has a black string to keep it closed, which I can also use to keep my place.

"You can write in this every day, after you leave here. It will be a way for me to be with you, even after you're gone."

"Thanks"

For the first time in almost three weeks I'm able to get a word out whole, in one shot. No stutter. I know it's a short word, but it is a *word.* I stroke the cover of the journal and smile at Dr. Zargis, not wanting to say anything else. *I'll quit while I'm ahead.* Dr. Zargis gives me tissues for my tears. "You're a brave and strong young man," he says. "You're going to be okay. You are going to be okay." He opens the door and I give him one last wave before he leaves. The door shuts behind him, but I know he's there. I know he'll always be there.

CHAPTER FORTY-TWO

"You will be just fine

at Our House. You will be able to continue your rehabilitation, and you'll have access to our counselors and our on-site therapist. Even though it won't be like your home, we like to say *Our* House can be just like *your* house."

I seriously hope not, for real.

I-I-I-I-I-I

"don-don-don don't waaaaa-nnnna go. Nnnnnoooooo."

"I'm so sorry, Jayson I know it must be hard for you right now, but I'm afraid there really isn't any other choice. Just try to relax, and trust me when I tell you that you'll be living in a safe and supportive environment, just what you need right now. It's just what you need. You'll do just

fine." Mrs. Williams gives me a pat on my halo and walks
out.

Our House is right smack in the middle of the 'hood.
Should be lots of fun livin' there. That area makes the
Gardens look like Park Avenue. *Yeah, right, lots of fun. Out
of the fryin' pan and into the fire. . . .*

Dear Trina

I know, I know you're my mom. Please help me. Please
come and get me. I need you, I really need you.

I fill up three pages
front and back. I tell her everything. Things I couldn't
even tell Dr. Zargis. How Mom hits and beats, what
happened to Trax, what happened to me. I tell her
everything.

Still There
The card, I had it in my suicide clothes, back pocket of
my jeans. Can't believe it's still there. Just barely able to
make it out . . . but I can. I copy down her address and
give my letter to one of the nurses to mail. *At least I tried.*

Outpatient Therapy
That's what they say is next, after I am released
tomorrow. Not just for my body, but for my mind,

too. Hooking me up with group therapy and weekly psychotherapy as well as PT, occupational, and speech therapy. Closer to where I'm *gonna* be living. *When will I have time for anything else? Who's gonna pay for all of this? I think they're just blowin' smoke, I'll prolly be lucky if I even see a physical therapist. Like they have all those doctors in the hood. . . . Just blowin' smoke, for real.*

CHAPTER FORTY-THREE

"See, what happened was . . ."
I know instantly that this isn't a dream. The voice, the smell. The lies. I don't even have to open my eyes. Bet she found out the cops were lookin' for her and came back quick. I bet she would've stayed gone if the cops hadn't been on her ass. Prolly got wind she was a missin' person. Came back quick—just like Lizzie. Always lookin' out for number one. Now she's talkin' some serious shit about how Lonnie's aunt was sick and they had to leave town on account of some shit—I don't even know what the hell she's talkin' about. Don't care, either. I wish the cops would have searched her instead of just lettin' her come up to my room like she was my *savior* or some shit. Man, I know they didn't search her, 'cause if they did, they would have found all kinds of drugs and who-knows-what else, *for real.* As bad as Our House sounded, I'm sure it would have been *way* better than Lizzie's House.

Fuck, I can't believe she came back.

Mom looks like

a bloated fish with a bad hairdo. Wearin' a faded pink
tank top that's barely coverin' her chest. She smells funky,
too, like she just got back from wherever the hell she's
been and didn't have time to shower. I can tell right off
she's been on a binge, for real. Always gets that puffy look
when she's been drinkin' real hard. Her eyes are small and
beet red too. *Prolly been doin' more than drinkin'.*

"I got it all straightened out"

"You're comin' home with me. Talked to that Mrs.
Williams lady and that one from Social Services. They
both said the best place for you is back home. Back home
with your mom. I'm so happy, Jay, I'm just so happy. It's
gonna be different this time, Jay. Don't you worry, I'm
gonna take real good care of you."

I bet you will. . . .

Good-bye

I say good-bye to everyone. Gary, my Abu Ghraib PT
dude, and Cindy, my speech therapist. And all the nurses
and techs and this new family that I've gotten to know.
Gotten so close with. The ones that bathed me, cleaned
me, wiped the shit off my ass. The nurses who held
my hand and said everything was going to be okay,

everything was going to be alright. Dr. Iram, who brought me back from the dead. Dr. Zargis, who shrunk my head, tried to get me to see that things could be okay. If I work hard and try not to forget the past, to learn from it but not to live in it . . . They think I'm on the right track. They really think that. They don't know Mom, I mean *really* know Mom. . . . They don't know what she does, what she's capable of. They don't know that she'll *never* get better. There is no halo that can fix her soul, there is no doctor that can cure her hate. How many times can you jump and survive? How many lives will I get? I really don't wanna find out. I don't wanna go home.

Please, don't make me go home. . . .

CHAPTER FORTY-FOUR

People stare

as I do my best Frankenstein imitation through the
Gardens lobby. I'm sure this walker makes me look like a
senior-citizen Frankenstein, but I don't think I could
walk without it. It helps with my leg and keeps me from
toppling over when I move. I pretty much got the hang
of the thing. At least inside. Not gonna be too good outside, though. I can see myself tryin' to get away from
some gangstas out on the streets. *Prolly put that on*
America's Whackest Home Videos, *for real.*

One month gone

but the smell of the lobby—the smell of the Gardens—
ain't. Been away from this place so long . . . but it all
comes back fast. That day, that second, that . . . I feel
tears start to fill my eyes. Lizzie doesn't even notice. The
elevator doors shut, I press eighteen, it smells like piss, we

start moving up. I want to hit seven, see the spot where
I—but I push the thought fast out of my head. The
elevator does its slow bumpy thing until it jerks us to a
stop. Out on eighteen I get a little dizzy as I walk onto
the breezeway. *God, I hate this thing on my head.* Lizzie
takes the keys out of her purse. I feel like running, if I
could. I wish I was back in the hospital, back with Dr.
Zargis. *I wish Trax was here.* I stand outside the door as
Lizzie walks in. I can't move, don't wanna move, don't
wanna go in, don't wanna go back to that life. Don't
wanna go back.

The first thing I see

is Lonnie's long-ass legs all stretched out on the couch,
like he owns the place. He sees me but it takes him a
minute to realize who it is. *He's prolly stoned.*

"Hey, boy, good to see ya. Glad you could join us. Man,
they got you all jacked up with that, that thing on your
head. Does that shit hurt?" *Same ol' sensitive Lonnie.*

Lizzie drops my hospital bag on the living room floor and
goes over to Lonnie, leaning down and kissin' him like
they haven't seen each other in years. I prolly could just
walk out the door and she wouldn't even notice. She's in
deep French-kiss mode as I walker my way to my room.
Lizzie doesn't even look up. Neither does Lonnie.

(Not) Just the way I left it

Looks like shit was moved, then put back all in a hurry. It's like she tried to put stuff back, but she didn't try that hard. I wonder if she thought I wouldn't make it. Maybe she was gonna rent my room out. I carefully lay myself on my bed, close my eyes, and try to figure out how the hell I'm gonna survive this. Thinkin' how I'm right back where I started from. Just one big fucked-up circle with nothin' gained and a whole lotta shit lost. . . .

I wake up #1

Still in my bed, but out of the corner of my eye I see Lizzie and she's hitting me with her fists, but now they start to bleed so she picks up a hammer and starts smashing my halo, hitting the pins, hitting my head. I can see bits of my brain on my bed. I pick them up with my hands. I pick up bits of my brain and throw them at Lizzie. I stuff them down her throat and choke her with pieces of my brain. I choke her until she gasps for air. Then I choke her some more.

CHAPTER FORTY-FIVE

I wake up #2

Opening my eyes all of a sudden. Sucking in air like I'd
been holding my breath. *Must have fallen asleep . . . What
time is it? Damn, that was a fucked-up dream.* I am glad my
halo is still attached to my head and my brain isn't on my
bed. But . . . *I'm still here with Lizzie, in this house. Nothin's
changed.*

Back to sleep

until . . .

The morning knocks

*quiet at first. Then louder and louder until it starts to give me a
headache.* The first few seconds that I'm awake I forget
what's on my head, so I try to get up like I used to. Yeah,
that doesn't work too good. The knocking feels like it's
rattling my halo. I want to yell, but I don't feel like

hearing myself stutter first thing in the morning. I get up slow, just the way they showed me. At least Mom got the right bed that I need. Rails on the side to help me get a grip so I can lift all this dead weight on my head. I lean against my walker; the first of the morning pain stings me from head to toe. I start for the kitchen, for a cup of water. *Gotta take my meds before I do anything. God, I wish they'd quit knocking.*

"I heard you were back home"
April walks into my apartment and tries to walk back into my life like nothin' happened. Like it wasn't no big thing that she never came to see me. I try to be cool, try not to show how I feel. I try to look mad, but I know I can't front. Damn, it's just so good to see her.

"You look good"
I can tell April is lying. I can see it all over her face. I can see the guilt, too. She looks twisted, conflicted—wishin' she could change the past. *I wish I could change it, too.*

What she doesn't say
is a lot,
is
"why?"

April's small talk
"Is it hard to move in that thing? Does it hurt? How

long do you have to wear it? When can you go back to school? I've been . . . *blah, blah, blah, blah, blah.* You really do look good. *Blah, blah, blah, blah.* You know I've missed you . . . *Blah, blah, blah, blah . . .*"

April looks scared

of me. Scared of the suicide boy, the kid who tried to kill himself by jumping from seven floors. *Anyone who tries that must be crazy.* I can almost hear her thoughts. No matter what she says, I know that's what she's thinking. Her body language. How she shifts in her chair.
It's all away, away, away
from me, from me,
from
me.

Now I know

why. All of a sudden it hits me. I know. I know why she didn't come and see me. She was afraid, she *is* afraid. She just couldn't handle it. Couldn't handle that I would do what I did . . . what I tried to do. . . . I'm not the same person to her.

It's just like what Dr. Zargis told me. *"Some people will react in a very strong way to something like this. They may never want to get close to you again."*

I didn't want to hear it then, but I know now.

234

He was right.

I haven't opened my mouth

I don't want her to know my speech is all jacked up. I
don't want her to know more than I *want* her to know. I
just try to nod and force a smile. Sometimes I look away,
sometimes I stare right at her. Sometimes I close my eyes
and wish none of this ever happened. . . . It's on me
quick. The *hurt.* Not from my injuries but from knowin'
that things will never be the same with April. *We* will
never be the same. My mind goes back to the last time,
that last time we were together. Now *I'm* feelin' guilty,
knowin' what I was gonna do that last time. Knowin' I
was gonna go try and kill myself right after we made
love. That wasn't right.

April is looking down as she talks, not looking at me at
all. I finally stare at her face, wishing I could touch it, kiss
her, feel her again. I smile for real this time, catching her
eye. She smiles back and, for a second, I think she looks
at me like she did before. For a second I think she's about
to tell me that she understands and she's okay with everything that's happened, and we can try to work it all out . . .
instead of having this real uncomfortable vibe we've got
going. For a second it seems like everything is gonna be
like it was . . . for a second . . . but then that second . . .

is gone.

She hugs

me *carefully* and says good-bye. She says she'll stop by again soon. I know she won't. "It-it-it-it's oh-oh-oh-oh kay," I whisper in her ear. I feel a tear run down my cheek. She holds me as close as she can, almost like she used to. *Almost.* I watch her walk down the breezeway, disappearing around the corner. I shut the door. The tears come in waves, but I don't try to stop them. I just let them come. I just let them come. . . .

CHAPTER FORTY-SIX

Lizzie is doing the bare minimum

Two weeks I've been home from the hospital and only
been to PT once. Only been to my shrink once, too.
Mom says I'll heal up fine. But it seems like she don't
care one way or the other. Seems like she's just doin'
what she got to, to stay out of trouble. Sometimes she
asks me what I talked about in the hospital. Prolly tryin'
to find out if I told anyone how much of a monster she
is. She hasn't blown up yet, but I'm sure she will. Just a
matter of time, only a matter of time.

In the elevator

on my way to my *second* shrink appointment. I feel like
screaming. It's like this everytime I pass Trax's floor. I feel
like pushing the emergency STOP button.

I feel like it's happening

all

over

a

g

a

i

n.

I'm scared

"Ah-ah-ah-ah lot. Affff raid of eeeeeev-ry thing.
Shhhhit." I try to tell Dr. Josephs how I feel. I get
frustrated 'cause I still can only talk in small chunks.
"I-I-I-I cccccan't doit. ccccccan't gggggo ttttt-toseven."

"When you're ready," he says.

"Wh-wh-wh when wh-wh-wh will I-I-I-I bbbbbbb
beready?"

"You'll know," he says, shuffling some papers on his lap
and looking down while he answers me. Dr. Josephs is
always doing like five things at once. I mean, he's
listening to me, but he's always looking at some papers
while he speaks, papers that don't have anything to do
with me. He never misses a beat, but still I wish he
wouldn't do other things when he's with me. Dr. Zargis
never did.

I am waiting for Lizzie

to pick me up. She's late. Outside in front of Dr. Josephs's building it's starting to get dark and my arms are getting tired from leaning on this walker. Anymore, I don't really need it that much around the apartment, but when I go out I don't want to take a chance on falling.

Lizzie and Lonnie

pull up in some car I've never seen before. Looks almost brand new. "It's my aunt's, who was sick. She's lendin' it to me till she gets better." Lonnie sees me eyein' the car so he tries to get the jump on me before I ask him about it. I don't even have to look at him to see that he's lying. I look over at Lizzie sitting in the passenger seat. Her eyes look wild, darting all over the place. She's sweating, too, like someone just threw a bucket of water on top of her head. She's wearin' a ratty-lookin' white T-shirt with what looks like a coffee stain on it and a jeans skirt that is *way* too tight and *way* too high. She's in constant motion as she talks. *Oh man, she's jonesin' bad. . . .* I knew it wouldn't take long before she was back on it. Two weeks of tryin' to go straight and that was enough. Now she don't even give a fuck how she looks to me. *This is not good.* Lonnie steps on the gas, and before I know it we're flyin' down the street. I am seriously worried that these pins attached to my head are gonna end up in my brain if he doesn't slow down. Lonnie is whisperin' somethin' to Lizzie as he drives. She nods. I try to keep my Frankenstein head as

straight and still as possible. Holdin' my halo to make sure
it doesn't go nowhere. Lonnie starts goin' even faster.
Man, they must be late for a drug deal. Fuck, that's all I
need is to be in a wreck and end up back in the hospital.
Be just my luck, *for real.*

The lights are on

I can see them as soon as we get to the front door.
Someone's robbin' us is my first thought, then I think about
it for a minute. *Who robs you with the lights on?*

"What the fuck are *you* doin' here?"

"You got some fuckin' nerve showin' up here, walkin' in
my house like you live here. You in *my* house. *My* house,
bitch. You think you're gonna leave here in one piece?
You crazier than I thought you were. I will fuck you up,
you know I will."

"I'll handle this," Lonnie says, pushin' Lizzie behind him.
"I don't know what you mean by comin' here. But you
need to leave. And *now.* If you don't, well, I can't say what
might happen to you. You understand what I'm sayin'?"

I am having that out-of-body experience again

floating in the air, high above the room, looking down.
Watching Trina, my *real* mom, about to get killed by the
monster and her boyfriend. Watching myself just standing

there, looking shocked, not able to move. Looking down at the poor suicide boy who just lets everything happen to him. Powerless, again. . . . *I have to get back down there. I've been up here too long as it is. I have to save her. I have to save my mom.*

"I just wanted to see him, the door was unlocked"

Trina's words are soft as she walks closer to me. She slowly puts her right hand out to me, then the left. "I, I know what happened." Now she carefully starts to hug me. Speaking even softer in my ear . . . whispering now . . . "I got your letter, baby. I'm so sorry, so, so sorry. Everything's gonna be alright now." Trina looks me right in the eye, speaking strong, clear—making sure everyone in the room can hear her. "It's okay, baby, Momma's here. Momma's back."

The Monster Screams

"Oh, so now you done went and told the boy. Real good, Trin, real smart. You are *not* his mother. I am. I don't care whose womb he came out of, that don't mean shit. I raised him. You didn't. And as far as the law's concerned, that boy's mine. You left him and didn't come back, 'cause you was a crack whore, plain and simple. Now you think you can just waltz back into his life? Over my dead body."

Trina's Calm

"You know what the truth is, Lizzie. *You* know it good and well. We both know. You took him, Lizzie, you stole him from me all those years ago. I tried, you know full well I came back for him, but you were gone. Then once I tracked you all down I made it my mission to see him, to at least talk to him. After all that time went by I knew it was best not to tell him the truth, at least until he got older. I had sense enough not to try to confuse a little boy. I just wanted to be a part of his life. At least a little part of his life. But you wouldn't let me. Well, let me take that back. When it came to givin' money or helpin' him get into a good school, you had no problem with that. Always a taker, Lizzie, you was always a taker. God help me if I wanted to write him or visit. No, you would have none of that. You threatened me, had me chased away whenever I got close. That last time, Lizzie, you remember the last time? Last August? You wrote me, told me to come visit. You said the past is past and it's time for us to be friends again, you remember? You said that finally we would tell Jayson the truth, that he could come back with me, just for a visit, just so we could get to know each other. *You* even said it would give you time to try rehab again. But after I spent just a little time with him, you lost it—you snapped, Lizzie. Then you went and had one of your gangsta friends put a hurtin' on me, real bad. I still have the scars. Lizzie, you want me to show him the scars? Do you? I've done everything I could for you, Jayson. I haven't had much, but whatever I've had I've made sure to give you what I could. If I'd known things were gonna turn out the way they did, I would have told you . . . God knows I would have . . . I *loved* you all these years, Jay, and I've *never* forgotten you are my son. Too much time, too much lost time. You gotta let go . . . It's time Lizzie, it's time to let go. It's time."

"I ain't lettin' go of shit"

"He's my boy. Always has been, always will be. You ain't gonna come in here and start spoutin' a bunch of lies. Actin' like you was some kind of angel or somethin'. Give me a break. You was a crackhead just like the rest of us. Don't try to act like your shit don't stink. Comin' in here, tryin' to turn my boy against me. Hasn't he been through enough? Look at him. I ain't gonna let you do this. It's gotta stop. It's gotta stop now. Playtime is over. It's time I taught you a lesson, once and for all. You fucked up, Trina. You should never have come here. Now you don't get to leave. You got to stay and get what's comin' to you. You ain't goin' *nowhere.*"

I Am Back

Back in my body. My mind is racing, thinking of all the things that might happen, all the things that could go wrong, and the one thing that could go right. The one thing I want the most. *My mom.* I turn to Lizzie. Now it's time to give the performance of my life. At least I don't have to fake the stuttering that should tug at the heart-strings. *If she has any.* "It-it-it-it it's oh-oh-oh-oh kkkkay, mmm Mom. I-I-I kn-kn-know yyyy you're mmmm mymmmmom. I-I-I lllllove you. Pppplease ddddon't hhhhurt hhhher. IIIII kn-kn-kn-know sh-sh-sh she's-lyin'." I walker my way over to Lizzie, going extra slow for the most effect. I give Lizzie my most pathetic look, holding out my arms to the monster. Giving her the biggest hug I can without falling over. I look into the monster's eyes for any hint of compassion. Any hint of sympathy. I squeeze tighter.

Lonnie gets a call

"Okay, cool," is all he says. He puts his cell back into his sweatpants pocket and taps Lizzie on the shoulder. "We gotta roll," he says.

Lizzie lets go of me so fast I almost lose my balance and fall. She races into the bedroom and comes back with her purse. It's half open, so all kinds of stuff is spilling out of it. She sprints back into the living room, right past me and Trina, straight to the front door.

"We gotta go"

"And I ain't got time for all this craziness. I ain't gonna catch no case on account of your nasty-trick ass. I got business to take care of, gotta provide for *my* son. I'm gonna give you a thirty-second head start to get the hell

out of here, before we take off. You lucky as hell, Trina.
Don't ever say I never did nothin' for you. Now get the
fuck out of here." Trina squeezes my arm and leaves—
quick, out the door. Mom and Lonnie whisper to each
other, and about a minute and a half later they're gone,
too.

I'd like to think

that it was my Oscar-winning performance that made
the monster give Trina a pass, but I know it wasn't. It
was the dope man callin', lettin' them know it was time
to get their stuff. Or maybe it was some druggie who
wanted to buy from *them*. They prolly' usin' *and* sellin'.
Wouldn't be surprised. All I know is that once that
phone rang, they could've cared less about Trina or me.
Could've cared less . . .

I am tappin' the kitchen table, lookin' up at the clock.
Only been ten minutes. Prolly makin' sure the coast is clear. I
know she'll be back. I know it.

CHAPTER FORTY-SEVEN

He looks terrible

but he's happy to see me. He looks like he hasn't slept in days. *Prolly been out on those streets for God knows how long.* He doesn't look well. His skin is real pale, and *he's so thin.* He's got on red shorts and a wife-beater T-shirt, lookin' like an anorexic Lennox Lewis. Tears well up in his eyes as he gives me a hug. A *real* hug. We sit down on his old torn-up couch. He listens without saying a word. He listens, nodding his head. Laughing, smiling—crying . . . then there is silence. No words are spoken. After a few minutes *that seem like hours,* he gets up and walks into the kitchen. I hear the faucet come on. He reappears, taking a sip of water from a jelly jar glass. He sits back down next to me on the couch. "It's the only way. It's the only way." He repeats this softly over and over again. Saying it under his breath, like a whisper. He puts his arms around me, holding me. Crying. I start crying, too. I look at this frail man, this man whose body is practically decomposing before my eyes, and I know as sure as I'm sitting here that I won't ever see him again. *Time to let go of the hate. It's time.*

He looks at me, takin' me all in, like, like a proud father. Through his tears he says, "I love you, son, I love you . . ."

"I-I-I llllove yyyyou, Ddddad. I-I-I-I llllove yyyou."

One last thing to do

I make myself. It's what I have to do. I walk slow to the spot, passing Trax's apartment. It's empty for now. Found out his mom left soon after the funeral. Not sure what happened to Tyler, hope he's okay. I touch his door, letting my fingers run across the numbers *Lucky* 777. The apartment next door is still being worked on. I can still see where the explosion—I start crying, but I don't try to stop. I know it's good for me. I know this will help me—heal. I walk over to the rail, looking straight out into the night. . . . For a split second I can almost feel what I felt—I think of Trax and hope he's okay, wherever he is. I smile through my tears. *Crazy-ass Trax.*

"It's time."
Trina's voice breaks into my thoughts.

I touch the rail and grab Trina's hand.

"I-I-I-I I'm rrrrready," I say to her.

"I-I-I I'm ready."

EPITAPH

CHAPTER FORTY-EIGHT

We are gone
like two spies leavin' in the middle of the night.

"You just let me know when you need to stop. We can
take as much time as you need."

Me and Trina. Goin' to Goner, West Virginia.

"Back where it all began," Trina says, gripping the
steering wheel tight, flickin' on her brights, then flickin'
them off. *Back to the start.*

Me and Trina thinkin' the very same thing. Right
after she came running back into the apartment
not fifteen minutes after Lizzie and Lonnie
left.

Me sayin': "I don't wanna stay."
Her sayin': "I ain't gonna leave you."

And that was that.

CHAPTER FORTY-NINE

"I moved"

"That's why it took me so long to get your letter.
Moved back to Goner, not too long after I sent you
that card. Been back and forth to that town half a dozen
times over the years. Always seems like it's where I end
up, no matter how far I try to get away from it. It pulls
me back.

"I'm glad it did this time, real glad it did. My God, Jay, if
I only knew . . . everything you've been through . . ."
Trina stops herself midsentence. I can tell she's tryin' to
keep from crying. She focuses back on the road, blinking
fast to keep away the tears.

"Once I got your letter, I left as soon as I could. Drove
nonstop to get here. Oh Lord, Jay, I'm so, sorry, I am
truly sorry for—for everything. I should have never left

you when you was a baby. I should have just toughed it
through. Should have never trusted *that woman*. Oh, my
sweet, sweet Jay . . ." Trina starts crying. I rub her back,
trying to calm her.

She shakes her head like she's shaking off her tears,
shaking away the past. "Suffer the children, that's what
the good book says. And Lord knows, you've suffered
enough."

There is so much
I want to ask. So much I want to know. About what
happened. To her, to *me*. So much.

But that will wait until later, until I have time to think on
it some more. To work on my speech so I can talk right
and clear, so there can be no misunderstanding about
what I'm saying, what I'm feeling. There is so much I
need to know—the details. So much I don't want to
know, either. So much.

"Wh-wh-what i-if sh-sh-she c-c-comes a-a-after us?"

"Don't care if she does," Trina says. "She'll never find us.
Goner's the last place Lizzie would think I'd take you.
She hasn't set foot in that place since we was kids.
Besides, she wouldn't spend the gas money to get there.

We both *know* what she spends her money on. And don't worry, she won't go to the police, either, the way she is and *what* she does.

"No, ain't nobody gonna bother us where we're goin'. And even if she did show up one day, she'd be on *my* turf. People still know me after all these years, some of 'em still call me Little Trin-Trin like they did when I was a kid. Yes sir, I am *quite sure* they wouldn't let no harm come to either one of us. I am *quite sure* of that."

Trina's tough
Not in a bad way, but tough, like someone who's had a rough life. Livin' on the streets, sellin' herself for money . . . gettin' hooked on drugs and alcohol. Had pretty much the same life as Mom, but turned out a completely different person. Trina got herself straight. Got herself together, for me. Back in the day *I* was *her* inspiration to get better. Now, *she's mine.*

I roll down my window and stick my hand outside
lettin' it get pushed up and down by the fast-movin' currents of air. I close my eyes and let the rush of the wind swoosh in my ear. My mind goes back to the past. To me and Trax, dancin' to Kanye West at Trax's apartment, tryin' to rap along to the songs. Trax spinnin' on

the floor tryin' to break dance, old-school style, actin' the fool. Both of us laughin' our asses off . . .

I can close my eyes and feel like Trax is right here in this car. I think I hear his voice, but I know it's just in my head. *I know he'll always be with me. . . .*

I think about what's happened. What happened to Trax, what happened to me. I wish Trax was with me in this car.

Before I know it, tears are falling down my cheeks faster than I can wipe them away. Trina reaches over and squeezes my hand, putting mine inside of hers, not letting go. "I love you Jay-Jay and I always will. You're goin' home, baby. You're finally goin' home."

Three a.m.
and Trina ain't *even* tired. "I got a second wind," she says.

Mile markers and exits are just quick flashes of light in our rearview mirror. I look over at Trina and I see strong and tough behind the wheel. I know that can be me, too. *One day.*

Three a.m., I want to close my eyes and sleep, but I'm afraid. Afraid I might wake up back in Bandon. I know that won't happen, but I'm still afraid. I prolly won't feel

safe until we get to Goner. You can never underestimate
Lizzie. She's just crazy enough to try to come after me.
Maybe she's following us right now.

I shake off the thought and try to take a deep breath—try
to let go. I try to let go of the past, let go of Bandon and
all the bad that's happened there.

Whatever doesn't kill you makes you stronger.

I remember Lizzie sayin' that to me when I was a little
kid. The one thing she was right about.

*I do feel stronger. Just by survivin'. I am stronger. Will get
stronger still, I hope. . . .*

Miles start to separate me from my *first* life. From The
Gardens and Lizzie and the man I called Dad. Even from
Trax.

It's that *first* life I want to forget. That life where everything I thought was real was a lie. That first life—
where I died.

I am still dead

and I'm glad. That dude I used to know? That *old* Jayson
Porter? Yeah, he was barely livin', just hangin' on by the
thinnest piece of thread.

Yeah, I'm glad he's dead. Buried his ass the moment
Trina—*my mom*—came back for me.

Yeah, I'm glad he's dead. I ain't got no feelings left for
that dude. I ain't got the strength for no more funerals.
Ain't got the *wherewithall* for no more hurt. Tired of
lookin' down into the black. Looking down into that
mean face of Hell. Trina set me free, but now the real
work starts. Have to rebuild after the storm. See what I'm
really made of. Gotta be more than just these broken-up
bones. It's up to *me* now.

Can't nobody save you from yourself.

Another Lizzie-ism. She's the poster child for that line,
for real. It's true, though. Can't *nobody* save you if you
don't wanna be saved. That's why I died.

But I was *lucky*. I got another chance.
I got another
life.

I see headlights come and go
Getting bright then fading. My eyes getting heavy. I blink
to keep them open, but it's a losin' battle.

I hear voices as I drift off to sleep. Some I recognize,
some I don't. Tellin' me to just rest. Tellin' me *"Momma's*

here now" and *"everything's gonna be alright."* I hear the sounds of passing cars and the radio turned down low. Trina is humming softly. . . .

I dream about Trax and Lizzie—*monsters at my door* . . . the hospital and bright white lights. I dream about being in April's arms—holding me tight. . . .

I feel myself sliding in my seat. My eyes pop open.

"Sorry, baby, some big trucker just got a little too close. Go back to sleep, honey, you need to rest. We've still got a *long* way to go. . . ."

I feel Trina put her foot on the gas, gunning it past another eighteen-wheeler. My eyes shut again as I feel my body drifting, slipping back into sleep. . . .

Still got a long way to go . . . A long way to go.

Special thanks to Mr. Terry Johnson,
for his invaluable research assistance,
and to my family, for all their
love and support.